D0710825

The Journey Begins

The Journey Begins

Storybook written by

Dennis Adair & Janet Rosenstock

Based on the Sullivan Films Production
written by Heather Conkie
adapted from the novels of

Lucy Maud Montgomery

HarperCollins*PublishersLtd*

The Journey Begins. Based on the Sullivan Films Production produced by Sullivan Films Inc. in association with CBC and the Disney Channel with the participation of Telefilm Canada adapted from Lucy Maud Montgomery's novels.
Teleplay written by Heather Conkie. Copyright © 1989 by Heather Conkie.

Storybook written by Dennis Adair & Janet Rosenstock. Copyright © 1991 by HarperCollins Publishers Ltd, Sullivan Films, Inc. and Ruth Macdonald and David Macdonald.

No part of this publication may be reproduced, stored in a retrieval system or transmitted, in any form or by any means, without the prior permission of the Publisher, or in the case of photocopying or other reprographic copying, a license from Canadian Reprography Collective. For information address HarperCollins Publishers Ltd, Suite 2900, Hazelton Lanes, 55 Avenue Road, Toronto, Canada M5R 3L2.

Design by Andrew Smith Graphics Inc.

Canadian Cataloguing in Publication Data

Adair, Dennis, 1945-
  The journey begins

(Road to Avonlea; #1)
Based on the t.v. series: Road to Avonlea.
ISBN 0-00-647033-5

I. Rosenstock, Janet, 1933- . II. Title. III. Series.

PS8551.D35J6 1991   jC813'.54   C91-093301-4
PZ7.A33Jo 1991

---

91 92 93 94 95 OFF 10 9 8 7 6 5 4 3 2 1

Chapter One

"Come along," urged Nanny Louisa. "You're daydreaming, aren't you?"

Sara Stanley walked by her nanny's side. It was a glorious, wonderful day, the kind of day that comes only in late summer. The lawns of Westmount, the district in Montreal where Sara lived with her father, all appeared neatly groomed, their hedges cut to perfection and their well-kept flower beds filled with late-blooming summer blossoms. Sara's eyes fell on the rows of brightly colored chrysanthemums, which waved on their long stems like ballerinas.

"I was just thinking of waltzing flowers," Sara confessed.

Nanny Louisa smiled. "The things that come into your head always surprise me, Sara Stanley."

Sara's nanny knew her to be an imaginative girl, given to flights of fancy and romantic daydreams. Others who knew twelve-year-old Sara Stanley either envied or pitied her.

"A poor, lonely child," one acquaintance sighed each time she saw Sara with her nanny.

"A spoiled child who spends much too much time with adults," whispered another.

"She should have playmates," insisted still another.

"Imagine taking a child to Egypt! It's a scandal. Who knows what she might see in a place like that?" one maiden lady huffed.

Those who pitied Sara Stanley knew she traveled a great deal, that she had few friends her own age and that, above all, she was a child whose mother had died when she was only three. Those who envied her thought Nanny Louisa tended to Sara's every need, that Sara's father spoiled her and that far, far too much was spent on her clothes, toys and tutoring.

The truth was harder to find. Sara was a mystery to many people, and sometimes she was a mystery even to herself. One minute she felt confident and brave, the next a little frightened and unsure of herself.

Sara and Nanny turned onto Victoria Avenue, a grand street lined with old maple trees which shaded the sidewalk from the late August heat. The ladies and gentlemen strolling along were stylishly dressed. The women wore wonderful summer straw hats trimmed with satin bows and delicate, handmade silk flowers from Spain. Many carried frilly parasols, and all of them wore the scent of flowery sachets, *eau de cologne* or fine perfume.

Sara gave Nanny's hand a squeeze and skipped on ahead. Nanny was a small woman, and because she was small, as well as elderly, she walked slowly, far too slowly for Sara, who felt the urge to run.

"Don't go too far," Nanny Louisa cautioned. "You just slow down and come back here, Miss Sara," Nanny called out. She grasped the straw bonnet that sat precariously atop her large gray bun. Wisps of hair escaped and caressed her forehead, and her little glasses slipped over her nose as she bustled along.

Sara stopped and waited for her to catch up. When she was younger, Nanny Louisa had played with her, instructed her and taken care of her. But now Sara wanted to do things for herself. As much as Sara loved her, Nanny Louisa was always lecturing, and she lectured more when they'd been shopping, as they had today.

"I hadn't finished talking to you," Nanny scolded. She shook her head. "Buying that dress was sheer extravagance."

Sara smiled sweetly. "Oh, Nanny Louisa, please don't fuss so! You know Papa promised I could choose my own dress. Besides, the shop girl said it's the color of moonlight...silvery and shimmery. Couldn't you just imagine yourself in a dress the color of moonlight?"

"Humph! As if moonlight had a real color," Nanny muttered. "Besides, were there such a color—which there isn't—you could see right through it because it would be transparent. The color of moonlight, indeed! I don't know where you get your romantic notions. No, I can't imagine myself in such a dress. And make no mistake, Sara Stanley, there's nothing less becoming than a young lady with puffed-up airs."

Sara wanted to say that she *could* see the color of moonlight in her mind's eye, but it didn't matter. Nanny Louisa's lecture went right in one ear and out the other. As they approached their grand house, Sara could see her father's shiny new electric Packard parked in the circular drive.

"Nanny Louisa! Look! Papa's home!" Sara ran towards the house, her heart pounding with anticipation. How wonderful it would be when she was old enough for Papa to take her on all his business trips. How grand never to have to stay home only with Nanny Louisa. Not that they didn't travel together now. But Sara did not think vacations were enough. She wanted to be with her father all the time.

"Sara! Now you wait for me. Do you hear?"

Nanny's voice was a distant sound as Sara tore down the street and into the wide, circular drive. In his stiff, black uniform, the chauffeur, Charles, stood beside the Packard holding a polishing cloth.

"Good afternoon, Miss Sara." Charles bowed his head.

"Good afternoon." Sara bolted past him. She stopped short at the front door. Two men were coming out. They had long, grim expressions on their faces, rather as if they had just eaten a jar of sour pickles. Behind them, Emma, the maid, stood dabbing her eyes and nervously running her hand over her dark skirt.

"Thank you, Miss," one of the men said to Emma.

"Good day, Sir," Emma managed to respond.

It sounded to Sara as if Emma had something caught in her throat. Why was she crying? Perhaps these strange men had come to give poor Emma bad news. "Are you all right?" Sara asked.

Emma nodded.

"Where's Papa?" Sara was breathless.

"In his study, Miss Sara, but you mustn't—"

Sara swept past Emma and ran down the corridor toward the winding staircase that led to her father's second floor study.

Nanny Louisa finally reached the front steps. "That child is irrepressible," she said, smiling. Emma still stood in the doorway, her face ashen, tears running down her cheeks.

"Whatever is the matter?" Nanny Louisa asked, putting her hand on Emma's arm.

Emma pressed her lips together. "Oh, you haven't heard the news? It's dreadful. I don't know what's going to happen."

Nanny Louisa frowned. "Do stop crying," she said primly. "Now, come into the parlor and tell me what's happened. Tell me slowly and rationally. Crying never helped anything. It stuffs up your nose and makes your eyes red.

It's unattractive and I'm sure it's unnecessary."

Emma looked into Louisa's stern face and burst into even louder sobs. "Terrible! It's terrible. What will become of us? What?"

Chapter Two

As Sara hurried to welcome her father home from England, she could not have guessed that, at this very moment, he was facing the most difficult moment of his entire life.

She flung open the door of his huge study. The great leather chair—his favorite—was empty, and a strange man stood by its side. He was a tall man, and he wore a dark suit. He had thin hair and wore a serious expression on his angular face.

There were two other men as well, whom Sara recognized. They were sitting in the three straight-backed chairs in front of her father's massive, highly polished mahogany desk. One had a handlebar mustache and the other wore funny little glasses and had a beard. But it was her father who seized Sara's full attention. He looked tired and worried, and she ran to him, concerned.

"Papa! You're back! I've missed you so much!" She buried her face in his chest, then looked up. "Is everything all right?"

Blair Stanley forced a smile. "Sara! It's wonderful to see you, my darling."

"How was England, Papa?" Her father put his arms around her and gave her a big bear hug.

Whatever it was these guests wanted, they would surely understand. After all, her Papa had been gone for a long time and they had missed each other. Her mother had died when she was three and she had no brothers or sisters. It was just she and Papa...and Nanny Louisa, of course. Only with her father, though, did Sara share the wonderful, secret, mysterious world of her imagination. Only her father understood her dramatic qualities, her desires, her dreams. And only she understood him. He was a gifted, sensitive and creative man. He was handsome and brave, too. In Sara's eyes, he was all the best things a person could be. She loved him fiercely and knew in her heart that they needed each other.

"Oh, Papa." Sara returned his hug. Tonight everything would be as it should be. Papa would sit in his favorite chair, she would sit in his lap and they would read together, as they had on so many happy evenings. He read to her

from *St. Nicholas Magazine* and from Grimm's
Fairy Tales and Hans Christian Andersen—wonderful stories about fairies and elves, about
kings and queens, princesses and princes. Now,
though, more often then not, it was she who
read the stories. "You read with great expression," he told her. The compliment made her try
harder. Now, each story she read was like a play.
She imitated voices, she became the characters.
Tonight, she would act out a fine story, a new
and special one to read to him on his return.

Her father released her from his arms and
smiled. "Sara, you know Mr. Bartholomew, my
lawyer, and Mr. Heinrich, my vice president."

"Hello." Sara smiled, trying to appear warm
and friendly, as she was certain her Papa would
want. But goodness, they all looked so serious.
Then she remembered Emma, who had been crying, and a feeling of foreboding flooded over her.

Mr. Heinrich shifted his weight from one foot
to the other. His face was flushed. "Hello, Sara.
My, haven't you grown!"

He always said that when he saw her. It was
rather a silly comment, since he saw her only
every six months or so. She was bound to grow.

"And this is Mr. Stewart," her father intro-
dued the gentleman standing by the leather chair.

"I'm pleased to meet you, Mr. Stewart," Sara said politely.

But Mr. Stewart didn't seem very polite. He simply nodded.

Sara looked up at her father. His brow was knitted in a frown. "Sara, I'm afraid I can't talk to you right now. And I'll have to work late tonight."

Did this mean her story would have to wait? Sara searched her father's troubled eyes. He couldn't hide anything from her. She *knew* something had happened.

He rose and stepped to the door of the study. "Louisa," he called. In seconds, Nanny Louisa appeared. Then he turned back to his daughter. "I'm sorry, Sara. Something—something has happened and it requires my attention."

"But Papa—"

"I'll be in to see you later, my darling. We'll talk before you go to sleep. Now you go off and have your tea like a good girl."

Sara frowned. It was only afternoon. Was Papa going to stay closeted with these grim-looking men for hours and hours? Her father looked pleadingly into her eyes. "Please, Sara. Go with Nanny Louisa."

She hesitated, because whatever was wrong

she wanted her father to share it with her. But she yielded to Nanny Louisa, who had gently taken her arm.

Before she left she turned and kissed him. "Promise you'll come later."

He bit his lip and nodded. "I promise, Sara."

Blair Stanley waited until the heavy door was closed and he knew Sara couldn't hear. Then he returned to his desk and sank into the chair behind it. He covered his face with his hands and wondered, silently, how events could have taken such a terrible turn.

Regaining his composure, he looked up at his somber companions. "I don't understand any of this. What do you mean you can't find Abernathy anywhere?"

Lawrence Abernathy was an accountant, the man he'd placed in charge of the finances of Stanley Imports. He had trusted Abernathy above all others. Apparently, it was a trust misplaced.

Gordon Bartholomew rubbed his chin thoughtfully. "Your Mr. Abernathy has simply disappeared, Blair. Vanished."

"Stanley Imports has been sucked dry," Mr. Heinrich added. "He didn't just take your money, Blair. Abernathy appears to be an experienced embezzler. He's been wily enough to put you alone in the seat of suspicion. There are pre-paid orders for expensive imported furnishings and works of art. Valued customers didn't receive their goods, nor were suppliers paid."

"And a good many of the customers were large stores, some of them publicly held companies," Bartholomew added.

"There's bound to be a lot of press—especially once the news hits the stock market," Heinrich added.

"I've employed Abernathy for years...I trusted him implicitly." Disbelief was evident in Blair Stanley's voice. He shrugged and shook his head. "Well, I'm afraid you'll have to deal with this, gentlemen. It's imperative I go to Toronto next week. I can't cancel."

The third man, Mr. Stewart, who had remained silent, stepped out from behind the leather chair and approached Blair's desk. "I'm afraid you don't understand the conditions of your bail, Mr. Stanley." He spoke calmly, flatly. "You *are* under house arrest. You can't go anywhere."

Blair Stanley looked up into Stewart's eyes, as the terrible implications of his situation began to hit him. Events had moved swiftly that morning in court. Bartholomew had spoken to the judge and assured him there was no question of failure to meet responsibility. Finally, he'd been released when Bartholomew had signed the necessary documents...bonds and the like. Blair's eyes sought Bartholomew now, and Bartholomew nodded silently.

"House arrest," Blair said in a slightly shaky voice. It sounded so dreadful, and immediately he thought of Sara. How could he keep this from her?

Chapter Three

That night, as Sara lay in bed waiting for her father, Nanny Louisa tiptoed down the darkened hall. She thanked heaven that the carpet was thick enough to muffle the sound of her footsteps, and she prayed that the dishes on the tray she carried would not rattle and shake.

Louisa stopped outside the study. From under the closed door, she could see the triangle of light that shone from Blair's desk lamp. Cautiously, quietly, she opened the door, balancing the tray in one experienced hand. She slipped inside.

Blair looked up. Strange, he admitted, he'd never really noticed how old Nanny Louisa was...nor till this moment had he thought about her age. But tonight, dressed as she was in her all-encompassing dark velvet dressing gown, with her gray hair knotted firmly atop her head, she *did* look older than he usually thought of her. Certainly, he reminded himself, she must have been close to sixty when Ruth, his wife, died nine years ago. Louisa had been his own nanny, but he couldn't remember how she'd looked in those days. She'd always been there. She was someone he took for granted.

How kind she really was, she'd brought him some dinner. He looked at her and shook his head and waved his hand. "No, please, Louisa dear. I'm really not hungry."

"You've got to eat," Louisa said firmly. It was a tone of voice he knew well. She often spoke to Sara in that same tone, and heaven knows she'd used it with him when he was a boy. Louisa was strict, yet warm. She was an old willow that could bend, and she was ferocious in her protection of him and of Sara.

She lifted a sharply arched brow. "You're cranky when your stomach's empty. Even as a boy, the moods you would get yourself into..."

"Now, Nanny Louisa, don't fuss," he said wearily.

She set the tray down in front of him and leaned over the desk. "Now," she said, as if he were still ten years old himself, "I want you to tell me what's going on, Blair Stanley. Emma and Cook are downstairs still caterwauling about bankruptcy and house arrests and goodness knows what else!"

He looked into her eyes. They weren't as blue as they had once been, and he knew she didn't see as sharply as before. As firm as her voice was, though, her eyes were not accusative, they were concerned. Strangely, her questions gave him comfort. He could count on Louisa to be level-headed. She was the most level-headed woman alive. Almost too level-headed.

"Well?" she said, questioning his silence.

"I'm afraid I put too much trust in my accountant, Mr. Abernathy."

Louisa folded her arms defiantly. "Humph! So, Mr. Abernathy turned out to be all show and no substance, did he? I never trusted that two-faced philistine! Does this mean that what I hear downstairs is true?"

Blair nodded. "I returned from England and was presented with a warrant for my arrest."

"Arrest? You're a man with a fine reputation. Surely no court of law will listen to his word against yours."

"I'm afraid it's not a matter of words. Abernathy covered his tracks. He's taken the money and disappeared. I'll have to make good on everything...it will ruin me." Blair shook his head as if he didn't quite believe his own words.

"Do you have enough to settle the claims held against you?"

"Probably not, Louisa. I may go to jail."

Louisa let out a long breath, as if she'd been holding it in. "Oh, Blair, it's bad enough for you, but what about Sara?"

Blair looked up at her intently. "Sara is troubling me most. She has to be protected from this at all costs. I don't want her dragged through something she's not old enough to understand. It's true I have many hard decisions to make about the business, Louisa, but what *shall* I do about Sara?"

Louisa turned and walked slowly over to the empty, cold fireplace. "Yes, she must be protected. Sara must go away for awhile. Until your innocence is proven."

"That would be ideal. But where could she go? I'd gladly send the two of you to Europe, but there's no money."

Nanny Louisa paced before the fireplace, then

suddenly stopped. "Didn't Ruth have relatives on Prince Edward Island? Yes, that would be perfect. Sara wouldn't be under scrutiny there. It's a million miles from nowhere, but quite pleasant, I understand."

Blair stood up defiantly, his voice almost exploding. "Over my dead body! I will never give my wife's overbearing sister the satisfaction of knowing my financial situation. She never wanted me to marry Ruth. You remember, I've told you about Hetty King. No, no, it's out of the question."

Louisa spun around to face him. She could be fierce too, and as she saw it, Blair didn't have many options. "Your pride is interfering with your common sense. Hetty doesn't need to know your situation. Simply cable her that you've been called away on a lengthy business venture and this would be a perfect time for Sara to get to know her mother's relatives."

Blair stared at Louisa. He drew in his breath, carefully considering her rather firm suggestion, and then nodded slowly. "I suppose that could work."

"This Hetty King may be an old tyrant, Blair, but she isn't Sara's only relative on Prince Edward Island."

"Hetty runs the family. She's the eldest. She

turned them all against me. When Ruth died, she blamed me."

"Swallow your pride, Blair. Think about your daughter. She must be taken out of Montreal."

Blair nodded slowly. "I suppose you're right. I suppose Sara might enjoy her cousins. Not that they're like my Sara."

Louisa smiled fondly, "No one is like our Sara," she agreed. "Now Blair, go to her and tell her what we've planned. Kiss her good night. I know she's waiting and she won't sleep a wink till you appear."

While Nanny Louisa and her father talked, Sara lay thinking and worrying about her father. She was reading, but at the same time listening. When she heard her father's footsteps she put down her book. "Papa?" she called as he quietly opened the door.

"Ah, you're not asleep."

"I've been waiting for you. Nanny said you'd come."

Her father smiled and sat down on the edge of the bed. He ran his hand through Sara's hair, brushing a few stray strands off her forehead. "I'm sorry I was so short with you this afternoon, Sara. I've had some bad news—a setback in business you might say. I'm afraid it's far too complicated to explain to you."

Sara looked at her father with concern. "Is it very serious trouble?"

He shook his head. "No, not at all. Just a little financial matter I hope will be cleared up within a month. But you won't notice the time. It will fly by."

"Fly by?" Sara questioned.

"Sara, I'm going to be terribly busy. And most of the business will have to be carried on right here in this house. I'm afraid it would difficult for both of us if you were about." He forced a smile. "You distract me, and the truth is, I just won't have time to be with you."

"If I'm not here, where will I be?" Sara asked, sitting up in her bed.

"I'm sending you and Nanny on a wonderful vacation to Prince Edward Island. You're going to visit your aunts, uncles and cousins." He leaned towards her. "Sara, you'll have a wonderful time."

"But what about my tutors?"

"Perhaps you'll go to school for a while on the Island." He smiled. "That *will* be an experience, Sara. It will be a grand adventure."

"I'd rather stay here. Oh, Papa, do I have to go?"

"My darling, I know this will all be cleared up soon."

Sara met his eyes. "We've always gone on vacations together," she reminded him.

Her father kissed her cheek. "I know, but I must stay here. I will send for you as soon as possible. You know I will."

"Do you promise?"

"I promise. Now you *will* make an adventure of this, won't you? Do you remember when we sailed the Nile and saw the Pyramids?"

Sara nodded. "Of course I remember. But we were together then. Oh, why can't you come with us?"

"I would if I could. I want you to enjoy yourself, Sara. You know how much Mama would have loved you to meet her family in Avonlea. Well, you're old enough now. It's fitting that you should go."

Sara tilted her head thoughtfully. "It will be interesting to be with a real family. I mean a big one with aunts and uncles and everything...won't it?"

"That's my girl," her father said, smiling broadly and slapping the quilt with mock enthusiasm.

Sara bit her lip. "I will miss you, Papa."

He leaned over and hugged her tightly. "Oh, how I'll miss you, too, Sara. I'll miss you every hour of every day."

"And you'll write?"

"Of course I will."

"And I'll write to you...I'll write every day."

"I can't keep up with that...perhaps every few days, or every week."

Sara kissed her Papa's cheek. "At least every week," she whispered.

For a long time after her father left, Sara lay awake, looking around her bedroom. How she would miss it when she was gone. By one window there was a comfortable window seat, and on either side of it were shelves filled with Sara's favorite books. Many of her "baby" toys had been put away, but certain items remained. A rag doll, a large ball and, of course, her rolling hoop and stick were things she seldom played with now, but still liked to have about. She had a wonderful little puppet theater, with four different backdrops and eleven hand puppets. She also had three dolls, dressed in satin and lace and high-heeled shoes.

Her pride and joy, however, was her dollhouse. It was two stories high, had nine rooms and was completely furnished in miniatures. In the grand living room there were even two tiny, hand-painted drawings in miniature frames. The table in the dining room was set with china dishes, and there was a miniature tea kettle on the stove in the little kitchen. "Quite the most wonderful dollhouse in all of Montreal," Nanny had proclaimed. "Not as fine as the one that belonged to the Queen of England, but close."

Still, Sara had to admit that the most wonderful dollhouse in the world couldn't make you happy if you were sad. Lately, she had been a little sad. She wished she could play without Nanny looking on...that she could have friends like other children seemed to have. Sara blinked into the darkness of her room. She *would* miss Papa, but perhaps going to Prince Edward Island would be an adventure. Perhaps Papa was right.

Chapter Four

The train crept through a pastoral landscape unlike any Sara had ever seen before. Not only were the houses few and far between, but the land itself looked as if it could have been painted by the great artist Vincent Van Gogh.

Yes, there was no doubt about it. The earth of Prince Edward Island—all the earth she could see from the train, including the dirt road that ran by the rail track—was bright red. It was so red it was a curiosity, and she wondered if one of her science tutors could have explained the phenomenon. The red earth made the grass look even greener, while the hillsides of wildflowers added even more color. The scenery was vivid, and the houses she saw were quaint, rather like the cottages inhabited by the elves in her story books.

"How unusual it is here," Sara remarked to Nanny Louisa, while continuing to look out the window. "Imagine how the moonlight must look when it shimmers on the sea and the hills."

"Desolate, if you ask me," Nanny Louisa concluded.

Sara ignored Nanny's comment. Nanny Louisa did not suffer change gladly, and she was always fussing and grumbling when faced with anything out of the ordinary. In Sara's eyes, though, the scenery was far from lonely. It was exciting and, more important, it seemed inviting. This *would* be an adventure.

Sara thought back over the past few days. It had all happened so quickly, and she still didn't understand why Mr. Bartholemew, and not her Papa, had escorted them to the station.

Sara looked at the seat across from them in the coach, where a boy, a little older than Sara, sat by himself.

For almost an hour Nanny Louisa had been scrutinizing him. He appeared to be about thirteen, with a strong and sturdy build. His unruly light brown hair kept falling over his forehead. After a time, she asked, "Are you traveling alone, child?"

At that moment, the boy grinned and opened his waistcoat. A small mouse peered out. "Except for Edgar," the boy said, indicating the mouse. No sooner had the words escaped him than Edgar, the mouse, popped out of his pocket and ran down the seat and across the floor towards Nanny Louisa.

Sara thought that in all her life she had never seen Nanny Louisa move so quickly. She shrieked and jumped up onto the seat, and Sara, stunned, did the same.

Hearing their screams, the conductor appeared almost instantly. "And what is going on here?" he questioned gruffly.

"This boy has a live rodent!" Nanny complained.

Sara, having recovered, announced, "This ruffian has frightened my nanny."

The conductor removed the boy immediately, but the mouse was lost. In the hours that followed, Nanny kept a wary lookout for Edgar. Finally she stood up, straightened her hat and advised, "We had better get ourselves together."

"So soon? Are we almost there?"

Nanny Louisa sighed deeply. "Oh, would that it were so! No, this train only takes us as far as Bright River. God willing, your mother's brother will pick us up there. What a frightful journey! My stars!"

Two porters knocked on the compartment door, and once admitted, began to take the numerous cases and hat boxes away. Nanny Louisa followed them down the corridor. "Do be careful," she warned. "Don't crush that large white box. Oh, do be careful...."

Sara followed in her wake, suppressing a smile.

The train jolted to a halt and the conductor swung down and pulled out the iron steps. The porters carried out the luggage. They had to make two trips.

"Aren't you going to put it in the station?" Nanny Louisa asked. Then, more concerned, "Where is the station?"

"Over there," Sara pointed. It wasn't really a station. It was merely a covered part of the platform, with a small part actually enclosed. From its red roof a big sign dangled which declared, in bold letters, "BRIGHT RIVER STATION."

The porters climbed back on the train and the conductor signaled the engineer. Sara and Nanny Louisa could not see him, but the boy who had shared their carriage—for a while, anyway—jumped gingerly from the very last car, darted across the platform and disappeared behind the station. Then, with a sudden bellow of the whistle, the train came once again to life and, like a great fire-eating dragon, chugged off.

"My stars," Nanny Louisa breathed. "There's no one here, not a single, solitary soul."

"But it is lovely, isn't it? It's so clear and the grass is so, so green." Sara's eyes scanned the scene and she breathed deeply as she smelled the sweet grass.

"It probably never stops raining," Nanny Louisa uttered darkly.

"You're just feeling grumpy again," Sara said brightly.

"And who wouldn't feel grumpy? We've been transported like sardines in a tin and now we're dumped like unwanted fish on a desolate dock. Train travel is simply not what it used to be."

"I'm sure Uncle Alec will be along soon."

"Punctuality is the sign of a gentleman. Well, no telling how long we may have to wait. We'd better get our luggage inside the station. In case it rains."

"There isn't a cloud in the sky!"

"Never mind. You can never be too careful when you're traveling. Come along, Sara. You'll have to help me."

Sara took one of the bags and Nanny Louisa took another. They made three trips between the platform and the station.

"We'll put it all right here," Nanny Louisa announced, piling all their luggage in a single stack, right next to the only bench under the station's roof.

That task completed, she was utterly breathless and collapsed onto the bench. She eyed their luggage and counted each piece. They had three carpet bags, three large basket cases and four hat boxes. Sara looked around the bleak little station and then sat down on the wooden bench, primly folding her hands in her lap. She had hoped there would be a little restaurant where they could have tea, but there was no such thing. In fact, there was next to nothing.

"A fine kettle of fish," Nanny muttered. "Here we are in the middle of nowhere and nobody to meet us. Where the devil is that Alec King?"

Sara looked curiously about while Nanny Louisa continued to complain. "What a dreadful trip! I thought that ferry would sink! I feared I'd meet my maker! Keep your hands on your bag, my dear. Thieves abound when you travel. You can't be too careful."

"Nanny, the station is quite empty. You needn't worry so much." Sara stood up and stretched, walking a few steps down the platform.

Louisa looked about uneasily and wondered if coming to this place had been a good idea after all. Born and reared in London, she had never lived in a rural setting. British to the core, she had certain standards and considered the entire North American continent, apart from Montreal and Boston, somewhat primitive. Nearly seventy, her long-ago memory of London had taken on a kind of mythic quality. "Coming here was the only practical thing to do," she murmured under her breath. But even as she said it, she feared the worst. "Well," she vowed, "if everything is not satisfactory, we will simply have to *make* it satisfactory."

Louisa shook loose of her thoughts. "Sara, don't you wander off," she called out. Then, to herself, "The only safe way to travel with young ones is to have them tied to you with a rope...a short rope." She steadied the hat box, which once again threatened to slide down the untidy mountain of luggage.

Suddenly, the boy appeared, rounding the corner of the station. He carried a tattered carpetbag and wore his cap slightly twisted on his head. He tipped it to Nanny Louisa. "Ma'am," he muttered.

"It's you!" she responded, frowning at him suspiciously.

"Did you find your mouse?" Sara asked.

"Don't talk to strangers," warned Nanny Louisa.

While Sara and Nanny Louisa devoted their attention to the boy, a large man parked his buggy behind the station, climbed down and headed for the platform. When he saw Sara and the boy, he grinned and said loudly, "Sara Stanley and Andrew King! I do believe that train got in a bit early!"

Sara stared at the man, then at the boy. The boy stared at her, then at the man.

The man laughed. "So here are the two long lost King cousins! Welcome to Prince Edward Island! I'm your Uncle Alec King."

Sara stared hard at the boy her nanny had called rowdy. Then, almost in unison, she and the boy both said, "Cousins?"

"And into the carriage with both of you," Alec King said cheerfully.

Sara paused. "And this is my Nanny Louisa," she announced.

Alec King looked at Nanny Louisa a bit strangely. But after a moment he mumbled that he was glad to meet her. Then he rubbed his chin thoughtfully and turned to Andrew. "What do you say, young man? How about helping me tie all this luggage on the back of the buggy?"

Nanny Louisa stared at Alec King. She wondered again if her suggestion that Sara come here had been the right one. The place appeared more primitive than she had thought it would be, and certainly Mr. Alec King did not look as refined as she had hoped Ruth's relatives would be.

"Ladies," announced Alec King cheerfully, "your chariot awaits."

"If only it were," Nanny said under her breath as she eyed the buggy.

Alec King helped Nanny Louisa into the buggy and then seated Sara next to her. "You'll have to sit up front with me," he told Andrew. "C'mon, let's go!"

They clattered off, and Nanny Louisa grasped Sara's hand for dear life.

"The luggage will fall off," she predicted darkly. "The buggy might even turn over. Oops! What a bumpy road. Do hold on tight Sara. Oops!"

Alec King turned slightly. "We've been expecting Andrew for awhile. My brother, Andrew's father, has taken a temporary job in South America. He spends his time looking for rocks, doesn't he, Andrew?"

"He's a geologist," Andrew said loudly.

Nanny Louisa smoothed out her skirt. "I was unaware of the fact that there would be another child staying with you. Let alone a ruffian!" Her nose twitched ever so slightly. "I do hope this won't make any difference to our accommodations."

Alec King laughed. "Of course not. I'm sure we can find space for you overnight."

Nanny Louisa sat up straight and rigid. "My dear man, what do you mean by overnight? I will be here for the duration of Sara's visit. Heaven help you if you don't have suitable accommodation!"

Alec King drew in his breath and vowed not to turn around. This Nanny Louisa seemed to

expect rather a lot. Well, it wasn't for him to deal
with this prissy woman. No: his wife, or better
yet his sister, Hetty, could deal with her. He
smiled to himself. Yes, Hetty would put her in her
place, and no doubt on the next train as well.

Sara wondered at her uncle's surprise that
Nanny Louisa was with her, but only for a
moment. So many new sensations were flooding
over her. She drew a deep breath and leaned
back in the buggy. The air was wonderful, and
the scenery! The ocean was blue and sparkled as
if diamonds floated on its surface. Green hills
gave way to golden hills of farms in the distance.
And the bright red earth she had seen from the
train seemed even redder now. Blue seas and red
cliffs, covered with green grass. "It *is* beautiful,"
Sara sighed. "Isn't it beautiful, Nanny Louisa?
Now I know why Mama loved her home so
much."

But Louisa was not to be mollified. After all,
she'd been brought up near the Thames and she'd
visited the famed white cliffs of Dover. "It's passable," she grumbled. "For the colonies."

Sara ignored her. It was more than passable. It
was her mother's home and it was wonderful.
Still, the people seemed peculiar, and she wondered if they would like her. She thought of her

Papa, wondering if he were thinking of her, and even as she thought of him, she felt sad and just a little lost.

Chapter Five

Sara craned her neck when they passed through a quaint and adorable little village. She spotted a white, spired church, a building with a sign that said GENERAL STORE, a pharmacy, a school, a newspaper, the Town Hall, the blacksmith shop and a livery stable.

"Avonlea," Alec King announced proudly.

It reminded Sara of the miniature village she had played with when she was younger. It was made of wooden blocks, and it even had little green wooden fir trees.

After a time, they turned down a winding, tree-lined road, and soon passed a little pond surrounded by trees and bushes. A large weeping willow looked as though it were leaning over and sipping from the pond. "How poetic," Sara sighed.

"I'd have missed the village of Avonlea if I'd blinked," Nanny Louisa said, her nose once again twitching with distaste.

In the front seat of the buggy, Alec King spoke

to Andrew. "Did your father ever tell you he almost drowned in our pond, Andrew?"

Andrew grinned. "He told me you dared him to swim across it, Uncle Alec. Is that true?"

Alec laughed and slapped his knee. He turned around and glanced at Sara. "If it weren't for your mother, Sara, Andrew's father wouldn't be alive today! Ruth jumped in, clothes and all, and saved him from drowning."

Sara smiled with pleasure. It was rather nice to think of her mother as a true heroine. "Really?" she asked, wanting to hear more about her mother. "I'd like to swim in the pond," she ventured. "It looks like a mirror, so clear and inviting."

"Swimming in ponds indeed! Lord knows what infections you might get," Nanny sniffed.

Sara didn't contradict her Nanny Louisa, but she wished at that moment that Nanny Louisa weren't such a worrywart. Once, when traveling with her father, Sara had seen a group of children playing together near a pond. He had called them urchins, because their clothes were dirty and they were playing unsupervised. Sara thought they looked happy, and she wondered how it would feel to run and play like that. She even wondered how it would feel to get one's clothes dirty now and again.

"Candy?" Andrew offered, fishing a boiled sweet from his pocket.

Sara reached for it, but Nanny smacked her hand. "There will be no sweets before dinner."

Sara withdrew her hand quickly. Nanny's smacks never really hurt. They were just reminders.

Sara took one last look at the pond before it disappeared from sight. A breeze rustled through the trees and over the sloping hills. The tall grasses seemed to be waving and a few ripples crossed the pond's surface. The breeze gently touched the willow, which shuddered. "I always imagined Mama buried near a pond that looked just like that one."

"As a matter of fact, your mother's buried not far from here. The King plot is just over that hill." Alec King pointed to a rolling hill lush with wildflowers.

"Just think, Nanny. This is the very same road Mama used to walk along. And look at the trees! I'm going to climb every one of them tomorrow."

"There will be no climbing of trees. Ladies do not climb trees," Nanny said, shaking her long finger.

Sara's eyes lingered on the trees a moment longer. There were so many things she had never done, things she wanted to do. As her mind wandered, the buggy clattered to a halt in front of a white farmhouse with a wide veranda.

"Well, here it is!" Alec King announced. "Welcome to the King farm." He grinned and pointed down the road. "Rose Cottage is at the end of this road. Hetty and Olivia live there." He turned and looked at Sara and Andrew. "Olivia and Hetty King are my sisters and your aunts."

Alec King climbed down from the buggy and Andrew followed. Alec turned and lifted Sara down, and then Nanny Louisa.

Sara clasped her hands together as she looked up at the house. "It's so sweet and small! It looks just like my dollhouse!" Sara never dreamed she might be insulting anyone, but unbeknownst to her, her cousin Felicity King had overheard. Just rounding the house, Felicity had stopped behind the bushes when the buggy drove up. "So small and cute," Felicity mimicked. "What was she expecting, a palace?"

In response to Sara's comment, Nanny Louisa only whispered, "It looks comfortable enough." Then she addressed Alec King imperiously. "Please see to the bags."

"Plenty of time," Alec muttered. This woman seemed to think she was the Queen of Sheba and in command of a thousand slaves. Well, he decided, Janet would deal with her. There would be plenty of time after dinner to tell the stuck-up nanny that there was no room here. In fact, it had already been decided that Sara would stay at Rose Cottage with Olivia and Hetty. He almost smiled. Mixing the arrogant Nanny Louisa with his authoritative sister, Hetty, should result in quite an explosive event. "We're home!" Alec King called out loudly.

Alec's wife, Janet, opened the front door and smiled, wiping her hands on her crisp spotless apron. Behind her stood three children. "Goodness, come in," she invited.

Alec and the three new arrivals stepped inside. Janet looked at Nanny Louisa with curiosity. "Hello," she ventured. "Excuse me, but who are you?"

"Miss Louisa J. Banks. I presume you're Janet King."

Still puzzled, Janet nodded. Nanny Louisa simply pushed by her into the main sitting room. Andrew and Sara followed in her wake, as did the other children.

"Who's that woman?" Janet whispered urgently to her husband.

"She thinks she's royalty, but she's only Sara's

nanny. She also thinks she's staying."

"Where in creation did she get that idea? I hope you made it clear we don't have room. Oh, the gall of that Blair Stanley. He hasn't changed a bit!" Janet fumed. "When he wrote to Hetty and Olivia about Sara he never even mentioned a nanny."

"Not now, Janet. Sara might hear you. C'mon, we'll straighten everything out after dinner."

Janet nodded and they followed the others into the sitting room.

"Well now," Alec King said, looking about. "It's time for introductions all around. This is Felicity, Cecily and Felix. And these, my children, are your cousins, Andrew King and Sara Stanley."

Felicity was a pretty girl, with golden hair and big brown eyes. Her younger sister, Cecily, had long, waist-length blond braids and a sweet face. Felix was round-faced and looked mischievous. Sara couldn't help but notice that the three of them stood close together, as if they didn't want anyone to enter their circle.

Sara followed Andrew's lead and stiffly shook hands with each of her King cousins.

"I hope you'll become good friends," Janet King was saying, but Sara wasn't sure. Felicity smirked at her and looked none too friendly. As for Felix...well, Felix made a face. He looked a proper brat, Sara decided.

Felicity, Sara soon learned, was thirteen and a half, and Felix, who seemed like a top that never stopped spinning, was eleven. Cecily was ten and really seemed as sweet as she looked.

"We're having lamb for dinner," Cecily announced. "You can sit next to me, Sara."

"We have to wash first," Nanny Louisa interjected. "I suppose you do have indoor facilities, don't you?"

Janet King shot her husband an angry look. "Just off the corridor," she answered briskly.

Sara looked at all their faces and felt uneasy. They didn't seem at all happy to see her. She wondered if they wanted her to visit at all.

Chapter Six

The buggy, still burdened with luggage, pulled away from the King farmhouse and back onto the dirt road that led to Rose Cottage. Sara sat primly in the back seat with her nanny. She hoped that her aunts Olivia and Hetty King wanted her more than her King cousins. An adventure—this was supposed to be an adventure, she reminded herself. Still, at the moment she felt unsure of just how things would turn out.

While Alec King took Sara and Nanny Louisa from the King farm, the three King children ran up to the room Felicity and Cecily shared, and fought for the best view of the departing buggy, from the small window overlooking the front of the house.

"Get out of the way, Felicity." Felix jabbed his sister with his elbow and pushed her aside. "You're too fat," he complained.

"You're the fat one," Felicity quickly responded. "Fat, and you have a great big fat moon face."

"They're gone," Cecily said. "You can hardly see them now."

"Where's that Andrew?" Felicity asked as she looked around suspiciously. "It wouldn't do if he heard us. I don't trust him."

"Unpacking," Felix said with dejection. "There's not going to be any space at all with him in my room. Did you see all that stuff?"

"He only had one little bag," Cecily observed.

"One little bag! It's a big bag and it's stuffed." Felix screwed up his face. "Heck, it's full of rocks and junk. And he keeps talking about the rocks here and how he's going to collect more. I'll be out in the barn before long and my room will be all full of big rocks."

"And the biggest will be your head." Felicity giggled at her own joke. Then she danced around the room, hands on her hips. "So sweet and small." Felicity again mimicked Sara. "Who does that Miss La-de-da think she is, anyway?"

"We hardly know her." Cecily's voice was soft. Her eyes still followed the distant wagon.

"Fancy thinking they could *all* stay here." Felicity ignored her younger sister. "Can you imagine having a nursemaid at her age?" Felicity paused, then turning to look in the mirror, ran her hand over her own cheeks. "And her complexion's terrible. I suppose that comes from living in Montreal. I've heard the air is dreadful there. We have pure air."

"You're being mean." Cecily watched her sister. "I like Sara, and I think Andrew is quite handsome."

"Oh, Cecily, you *would* say something like that. You'd think anyone was handsome...and they are, next to Felix," she teased.

"Look who's talking!" Felix made a face.

"No matter. Sara Stanley certainly isn't pretty." Then Felicity burst out laughing. "That hat she had on was horrible! She looked as if she was going to fall over, or take off in the wind."

"She's not pretty because she looks like you," Felix snapped. He always tried to better his sister, but somehow never quite succeeded.

Felicity made a face at him.

"I wonder what will happen when that Nanny Louisa meets Aunt Hetty?" Cecily ventured.

"Fireworks, like on Victoria Day! Skyrockets!" Felix rolled his eyes, then slapped his hands together.

"Imagine her telling Sara she couldn't drink tea made with pondwater! Imagine asking if we had 'indoor facilities'!" Felicity flounced down on her bed. "What did that old woman say when Mama told her she had to go to Rose Cottage? Oh, yes: 'We are not flotsam and jetsam to be moved about at will! Sara shouldn't even be out in the evening air! It'll be a mercy if she doesn't catch her death of cold!' Can you imagine?"

"I feel sorry for Sara," Cecily said, sitting down on her own bed. "She hasn't got a mother and her father's in some kind of trouble, and her nurse does seem strict."

"So she and Andrew have come to make *us* miserable," Felix concluded.

The door opened just then, and Janet King stepped into the room. "I thought I might find you three in here. Felix, you go right to the bathroom and scrub yourself clean." She turned to her daughters. "And when he's finished, you two do the same. It's time you were all in bed."

Felix did not hesitate. He darted away before his mother mentioned evening prayers or the never-ending need to practice his spelling.

"I wonder how it's going at Rose Cottage," Felicity said, smirking.

Janet suppressed a smile. The meeting of Miss Louisa J. Banks and Miss Hetty King was something she, too, was sorry to miss.

At that moment, the buggy halted in front of Rose Cottage. It was smaller than the farmhouse, but it had sloping eaves, window boxes filled with flowers and a lovely porch. It looked cozy and comfortable. It looked as a cottage should, nestled among the trees.

The first person Sara saw was a tall thin woman wearing a dark skirt and a severely tailored blouse. Her hair was pulled back so tight that not a single strand escaped. She had a long narrow face, with prominent cheekbones and sharp, dark eyes. She did not smile in greeting, but instead stood straight as a rod, holding a broom in one hand and looking as starched as her blouse.

After a moment, she stepped off the porch onto the steps. She craned her long neck and called out sharply, "Peter Craig! Where are you?" Then she took several long strides towards the buggy. "Hired boys are more trouble than they're worth!"

Before introductions, before a word from anyone, a young man raced round the corner breathlessly. "Sorry, Miss King. I was helping Miss Olivia with the chickens."

"So long as you weren't helping *yourself* to the chickens." She looked down her nose at him. "See those bags on the buggy? Well, bring them in the house immediately. Hurry up now, there's a chill in the air."

Sara smiled at the boy and he smiled back, but, clearly afraid of Miss King, he hurried about, following her orders.

Alec climbed down to assist Sara and Nanny Louisa.

Miss King stared hard at her, and for a moment Sara felt like an insect on a pin.

"So, this is Ruth's daughter." Hetty King said over the top of Sara's head to Alec. "From what I can see in this light, there's certainly more Stanley in that face than King."

Then Sara felt Hetty's bony hand on her

shoulder, and she looked up into her aunt's eyes. "Well, Sara...that is your name, isn't it? Since there wasn't room for you at the King farm, your father should be very grateful that Olivia and I agreed to take you in. We've put ourselves out more than *he* ever did for us. Mind you, I don't expect a thank-you."

Sara stared into Hetty King's face defiantly. Why was she saying such things about her father? Before she could speak, Hetty had turned to Nanny Louisa.

"And who might you be, madam?"

"My dear woman, I am Louisa J. Banks. Sara Stanley is in my charge."

Hetty scowled. "Not anymore. She is *our* charge now. We were not expecting you, so I'm sure you won't mind if Alec King escorts you to the rooming house in Avonlea. I assure you, you will be comfortable enough there until arrangements can be made for your return to Montreal."

Nanny Louisa stiffened like a board. "Pardon me, Miss King. I have been Sara's nanny since she was a babe in arms. I was her father's nanny as well. I certainly have no intention of leaving Sara."

Hetty arched her brow. "My good woman, this is not a hotel!" she snapped. With that, she turned abruptly and stomped up the steps, across the porch and into the house. The others followed.

They were standing awkwardly in the sitting room when Olivia King hurried in through the back door. She wasted not a second going directly to her niece.

"Sara." Olivia bent and hugged Sara warmly. "Oh, Sara! Let me look at you. You're the very image of our sister, Ruth."

Sara looked up into her Aunt Olivia's soft eyes. She appeared just as she did in the picture she'd sent last Christmas. "I'm glad to meet you," Sara managed.

Olivia turned around and, seeing Nanny Louisa, held out her hand. "Good evening... Miss—"

"Louisa J. Banks. And it is no longer evening, my good woman. This child should be well on her way to bed."

Olivia looked at Sara. "You are tired, aren't you?"

Sara nodded wearily.

"Hetty, we mustn't keep Sara up any longer. We can save our 'get to know yous' for morning, I think. Come along, dear, I'll show you your room. I spent days fixing it up for you. I hope you like it."

Nanny Louisa hurried up to Olivia as she guided Sara towards the stairs. "Excuse me, but I will see the child to bed."

Sara thought that Olivia looked a bit surprised. Olivia did not wish to be impolite, though, and was in fact a bit timid. "I'll show you the way," she said, allowing Nanny Louisa between them.

Hetty then stepped in front of all of them. "I've told you, there's no room here for you unless you want to sleep in the chicken coop."

Nanny Louisa was not to be intimidated. "If need be, I shall sleep on the floor of Sara's room!" she announced, and without further conversation, she edged around Hetty and flounced up the stairs.

When she reached the top, she called out her orders: "Bring our bags up immediately! Sara will have an egg, boiled for exactly three minutes, for breakfast...not too hard, not too soft. Do see that it is just right."

At the foot of the stairs, Hetty folded her arms across her narrow chest and looked at Alec King with narrowed eyes. She looked like a thundercloud, and mad enough to wring the neck of Sara's Nanny Louisa J. Banks. Hetty King was not used to taking orders. Quite the opposite. She was usually the one giving them.

Knowing his eldest sister as he did, Alec stepped back as if expecting an explosion.

"Alec King, you be here at seven a.m. That woman will be on the first train out of here without fail!" Hetty pressed her lips tightly together.

Alec King opened his mouth to speak, but saw the look on his sister's face. Clearly, Nanny Louisa's hours on Prince Edward Island were numbered.

Chapter Seven

Sara's room at Rose Cottage had a window overlooking the fields and the barn. "You can smell the ocean," Olivia told her when she showed Nanny and Sara the room. "And when the moon is up, it shines right in this window."

Moonlight and the smell of the ocean. It sounded pleasant, and Olivia seemed very kind. But everyone else seemed dreadful.

"It's small," Nanny sniffed.

Sara rather liked the room, although she said nothing. It had pretty flowered wallpaper and a bed with big quilts and fluffy pillows. Most interesting of all was the shape of the room. It wasn't exactly rectangular, like her room in Montreal, but instead was shaped more like a squashed square, with one wall longer than its opposite. She remembered that many old houses had secret passages, and that the passages caused the rooms to be oddly shaped. Sara wondered if Rose Cottage had any secret passages.

The bed proved too narrow for both Sara and Nanny Louisa, and for a time they tossed about trying to find a comfortable position. Then, Nanny Louisa got up and announced that what they both needed was a cup of hot tea to help them sleep.

Sara closed her eyes and waited in the dark bedroom while Nanny went downstairs. Soon, though, she heard loud voices, the loud voices of Nanny Louisa and Aunt Hetty. Olivia was there, too, but she spoke so softly that Sara could barely hear.

Sara crawled out of bed and went to kneel by the grate in the floor. It was there to allow heat to rise from the wood stove in the kitchen to the top of the house, but sound traveled up, too. Sara heard every single word, while her imagination created both the image of her outraged nanny and her stern, domineering aunt.

"I'd like to make Sara a little tea. Is there no

hot water in this house?" Nanny Louisa asked in irritation.

"There is if you boil it," Hetty replied sarcastically.

"Here, let me put the kettle on for you," Olivia offered. "It's no trouble at all."

"You *do* wash your dishes in hot water, don't you? They don't get clean otherwise," Nanny Louisa informed them.

"Of course we wash our dishes in hot water!" Hetty snapped angrily.

"I am only concerned with Sara's well-being."

"You needn't worry, we'll take good care of Sara. We'll care for her as if she were our own," Olivia put in calmly.

"Much as I wish we weren't saddled with the child in the first place, it is our duty to Ruth to see to her well-being. I for one am not a person to shirk my duty," Hetty said coldly.

"Oh, Hetty. It's more than duty," Olivia interrupted.

"It is *my* duty to look after Sara. I do not neglect my duty either." Nanny Louisa spoke firmly, as if to put Hetty in her place.

Sara listened and felt like crying. What was all this talk of duty? Didn't anyone actually like her? And why didn't anyone here seem to understand

Nanny Louisa? She *is* too protective of me, Sara admitted to herself, but that's just the way she is.

The voices from below grew even louder. "She is *our* flesh and blood. She is *our* responsibility. But another mouth to feed was not part of our bargain," Hetty announced.

"I assure you I can pay my way, if that's what you're so worried about." Nanny Louisa sounded as cold as Hetty.

"No amount of money would be enough to put up with the likes of you! Your airs and graces far outweigh your common sense," Hetty replied.

Even from her listening post at the vent, Sara could hear the bristling in both women's voices. Nanny Louisa responded immediately. "Mr. Stanley warned me about your hard-hearted ways! You turned your back on your own sister simply because she chose to leave this godforsaken island and marry him."

"That man dragged Ruth halfway around the world and back. He didn't give a second's thought to her health! Not a second!" Hetty replied in a loud, almost shrill voice.

"She accompanied him wherever he went. She did so gladly. She loved him."

"And she paid for his heedlessness with her life!" Hetty's voice was accusative.

"How dare you say such a thing? That man loved his dear wife with all his soul! Oh, he warned me about you. I didn't believe such a viper as you could actually exist. But now—now I see he spoke the truth."

"This is my house. How dare you speak to me that way in my own house! You will be leaving in the morning, if I don't throw you out first! Do you hear me?"

No one, Sara thought, could have failed to hear Aunt Hetty.

Again Olivia tried to intervene. "Hetty, really—things will seem so much clearer after a good night's sleep."

"I warn you," Hetty said. "If you don't choose to leave I'll tell the child the truth about Blair Stanley's situation and why she is here in the first place!"

At Hetty's words, a chill passed right through Sara. She listened even harder to the dreadful argument below. Something was wrong, something terrible.

"What do you mean, 'situation'?" Nanny Louisa asked.

"You know exactly what I mean," Hetty replied.

"He has a little financial matter to clear up,

that's all." Nanny Louisa insisted.

"Little financial matter, my auntie! Where do you think we are? Prince Edward Island may be an island, but it's not another world. We're still washed by Blair Stanley's sins. We're still left to pick up the pieces."

"I don't know what you mean...," Nanny Louisa stuttered.

"Well, let me read from the Charlottetown paper, then. 'Embezzlement Scandal Rocks Stanley Imports of Montreal. Chairman Blair Stanley Arrested for Theft'!" Hetty turned on Nanny Louisa. "So it's up to you, isn't it? Do you want Sara to have to face that scandal? Or would you rather leave Avonlea quietly and quickly?"

Nanny Louisa didn't answer. Instead, she turned on her heel and stomped out of the kitchen. At the sound of her footsteps on the stairs, Sara hurried back to bed and scrambled under the covers. She closed her eyes and pretended to be asleep, even though her eyes had filled with tears. Papa was in some terrible trouble and her mother's family didn't want her....

Nanny Louisa came in and quickly took off her robe, muttering and mumbling the whole time. "I won't spend another night with that dreadful woman," she vowed.

At that, Sara sat bolt upright in bed. "You won't leave me here with her?" she asked, tears running down her face.

"Of course not," Nanny Louisa answered. Then she turned towards Sara, her face stricken. "You heard, didn't you?"

Sara nodded. There was no use lying.

"Everything?"

"Yes, everything. Nanny Louisa, was the newspaper telling the truth?"

Louisa shook her head emphatically. "No. Newspapers never tell the whole truth, Sara dear." Nanny Louisa got into bed. "Go to sleep, Sara. Tomorrow is going to be a busy day...a very busy day. We'll have to get up very early...when the first chicken crows...we'll take our luggage and walk into town, then we'll get a ride to the train station. We're leaving this terrible place. So you just listen for the first chicken."

"Rooster," Sara said. "It's roosters that crow, Nanny."

"Roosters, chickens, never mind, dear. Just go to sleep."

Sara finally dropped off to sleep, but it wasn't long before she felt cold, and then woke up enough to hear the rooster crowing. The cold she felt was from the breeze that blows just before dawn, just as the sun appears on the ocean's horizon. Still sleepy, Sara jostled Nanny Louisa, and silently, and as quickly as possible, they dressed, packed their bags and tiptoed downstairs.

"On second thought," Nanny Louisa said as they reached the front porch, "We'll send for our bags later. Just leave them here. We can make better time without them."

"That's a good idea," Sara agreed. It certainly would have been folly to try to carry them. They could walk much faster without them.

They started out plodding down the road. Sara was rather sad to leave before she'd seen the orchard or had the opportunity to swim in the pond, or even run along the sand beach. But it was impossible. Aunt Hetty was a dreadful woman, and as nice as Aunt Olivia seemed, she couldn't make up for Hetty's nastiness. Besides, no one here except Olivia even likes me, Sara thought. Felicity seemed priggish and Felix was a wretched little boy. Cecily was sweet, like Aunt Olivia, and Uncle Alec and Aunt Janet seemed all right, but even they didn't really seem to want her there. After all was said and done, though, it all came back to Hetty. "She hates Papa," Sara said under her breath, "and I'm some sort of terrible burden for her...a duty."

"What?" Nanny Louisa asked.

"I said, Aunt Hetty hates Papa."

But Nanny Louisa wasn't paying any attention, because she saw that a buggy was quickly coming down the road behind them.

"Oh, what now?" Nanny Louisa asked as she halted in her march down the dirt road to Avonlea.

The buggy caught up to them, driven by Uncle Alec. "Morning Miss Banks. May I ask what you're up to?"

"Would you be so kind as to lend us your assistance in going to the main rail station, Mr. King?"

Alec King's face clouded over. "Now, Miss Banks, I can't do that. Sara's been placed in our custody. We're responsible for her and you must not interfere. This is a family matter."

At his words Sara felt a chill.

"I would sooner leave Sara with a nest of rattlesnakes than leave her here, Mr. King."

A very serious expression then covered Alec King's face. "Please be reasonable and understand the predicament you will cause if—"

Nanny Louisa stomped her foot. "If you won't take us to the station, then we'll just have to walk!"

"Oh, no you won't!" said Hetty King, who had suddenly appeared behind them.

Sara had a sinking feeling in her stomach. Hetty wasn't alone. She had a man with her, a most disheveled and untidy man, who looked as if he'd just been pulled from his bed.

"You see?" Hetty said, speaking to the strange man. "I knew she'd try to take Sara with her. We've caught you red-handed! Constable Jeffries! Do your duty!" Then, for good measure, Hetty turned and looked at Nanny Louisa hatefully and said, "You have to get up mighty early in the morning to put one over on me, Miss Louisa J. Banks, or whatever your name is. I went to get the constable before you even opened your eyes."

Then Mr. Abner Jeffries stepped forward. "I—ah, are you Louisa J. Banks?"

Nanny Louisa tossed her head in defiance. "I am."

"I'm the chief constable of Avonlea. It, ah, it appears we have a slight problem..."

"This is no slight problem, Abner," Hetty interjected. "This is a clear-cut case of kidnapping."

"Kidnapping?" Louisa said, looking aghast. "Are you mad?"

Aunt Hetty waved a bit of paper in the air. "I

received this telegram from Sara Stanley's father, Blair Stanley. It clearly states that we Kings are to be entrusted with the care of this child who stands before you! It is right here in black and white."

Mr. Jeffries then took a step towards Louisa. "Miss King here has proof," he said slowly, "in the form of the aforementioned telegram. It does say that this child is to be left with her mother's sisters. So, it is my duty as a humble representative of the court of law of Prince Edward Island to ask you to—"

"Get on with it, Abner! Don't be such an old windbag!" Hetty said impatiently.

"You have to leave," Abner announced.

"I'm not leaving without Sara," Nanny Louisa announced stubbornly.

Olivia came running up. She was wearing her heavy bathrobe, and her long auburn hair fell loose, tumbling over her shoulders. "What's going on?" she asked anxiously.

"Don't put Sara in the middle," Uncle Alec warned Hetty.

"Stay out of this, Alec. This person is simply an employee of Blair Stanley. She was entrusted only with the child's safe delivery to our door. As you can plainly see, she is about to spirit her away. I want this woman off my land and off this island!"

Hetty paid no attention to anyone, Sara thought bitterly. She even turned on her own brother.

"I am seeing Sara safely back to her father," Louisa protested vigorously. "because you're not fit to look after a dog, let alone a child!"

Hetty's face turned bright red, and she almost choked with anger. "Oh, and I suppose a household where the father is under arrest for common thievery is a healthier environment for a child than Avonlea?" she hissed.

"That's not true!" Sara cried out. Then she doubled her fists in anger. "How dare you say such a thing about my father!"

Alec straightened up. "Hetty, be reasonable. She is only here for a visit."

"A visit, indeed. Her father's going to jail. She'll be here till the cows come home."

Sara clenched her fists even harder and stomped her foot. "You're a pinch-faced, mean-mouthed old woman, and I won't listen to you!"

Hetty shot Louisa a cold, hard look. "So, that's how you let children behave in Montreal, is it? Well, a week in my care will take her down a peg or two."

Abner Jeffries took Louisa's arm. "Could we please proceed? If you persist, Ma'am, I'm afraid I'll have to charge you with the aforementioned kidnapping. If you leave for the train station willingly with me now, we can—let the whole thing drop—no harm done."

Louisa's luggage was fetched and Abner Jeffries borrowed Uncle Alec's buggy to take Nanny to the station.

Nanny Louisa stood up straight and said loudly, "I've never in my whole life seen such a mockery of justice! I am a Christian woman. I'll go, but you haven't heard the last of this! I promise you that!"

Then she turned and took Sara's shoulders. "I would not leave you for the world, Sara, but I have no alternative. I promise you with all my heart that I'll come back and fetch you once I have made other arrangements. Your father needs you to be strong. Make him proud of you, my dear. Be brave."

Hot, angry tears ran down Sara's cheeks. "No! I won't let you go! What about me? What am I going to do?"

"No one is going to harm you. It's all right my dear," Nanny Louisa said, trying to calm her.

Sara tried to cling to Nanny Louisa, but they

were separated. Then she ran into the house and up to her room, where she locked herself in and collapsed on the bed.

Why did her Aunt Hetty want to keep her? She didn't even like her. She tossed angrily and tangled up the sheet in both fists. Papa was under arrest...her mother's sister seemed like an old witch...Nanny was gone. It was as if the whole world had turned rapidly, and when it stopped, everything in her whole life had changed.

Now, twenty-four hours after her arrival at Rose Cottage, Sara lay on the bed and stared at the beamed ceiling of her room. This had been the most horrible day of her whole life.

There was a light tap on the door. "Sara? Sara dear, please come downstairs and have something to eat."

Sara sniffed and crossed her arms over her chest. Then she shouted, "I'll starve myself before I eat at the same table as that horrible woman!"

"Sara, dear. Please come downstairs. If you don't eat, you'll become ill," Olivia pleaded.

And then through the door she heard Hetty's voice. "You will hear no more begging from us, young lady. The larder is locked up after supper, so it will do you no good to try to sneak food at night. If you're hungry, there are berries in the fields."

Sara listened as their footsteps grew faint and they went back downstairs. She pressed her lips together and turned over on her side. "I won't give in," she whispered. "I won't."

Chapter Eight

Sara sat up and blinked open her eyes. The room still seemed unfamiliar, and each time she awoke from a deep sleep she had to ask herself where she was. In the pinkish, pre-dawn light she could make out the oak dresser and the wooden washstand, which held a white crockery pitcher and bowl because there was no running water on the second floor. On either side of the wooden washstand's flat surface there was a towel rack, and underneath was a shelf with extra towels and wash cloths, and a white dish that held a bar of soap.

There was a little desk against the wall, and on it was a green-shaded "banker's lamp" for studying in the winter when it was dark by four-thirty. The desk came with a ladder-back chair with a woven cane seat. There was also a more comfortable chair that sat by the window. It was covered in a yellow-flowered chintz material that matched the curtains.

Olivia had decorated and prepared this room, Sara thought a little guiltily. It wasn't as grand as her room at home, but it *was* cozy, and had she not been so miserable, she imagined she might have found it cheerful.

Sara liked her Aunt Olivia. Certainly she could not blame Olivia for Aunt Hetty's hateful actions and harsh words. Olivia was an angel, and Hetty was an old witch! Sara shivered and pulled the quilt up around her. She wondered if her mother had used this hand-stitched quilt, or perhaps even helped to make it.

After a few minutes she rubbed her eyes, which were full of sand because she'd been crying. Well, there was no use crying now. Nanny was gone and she was alone. And hungry. She'd hardly eaten anything on the train, hadn't eaten much for supper at the King house, and hadn't eaten at all yesterday. No matter how hungry I am now, or how hungry I get, I won't eat at the table with that woman! Sara vowed. She frowned and thought...Hetty had said there were berries. There was an orchard, too. Perhaps some of the apples were ripe. The more Sara thought about sweet berries and a ripe juicy apple, the more aware she became of the hunger pangs in her stomach. She would pretend she was Robinson Crusoe stranded on a desert isle...she would have to find her own food. I'll make a game of it, she thought. This is, after all, the very first time I've ever had to provide for myself.

For a long moment Sara sat in bed with the covers up to her chin while she planned every move. It was imperative to dress quickly so as not to get a chill. It was equally imperative to be absolutely silent so as not to wake Aunt Hetty. I will not give her the satisfaction of knowing how hungry I really am, Sara determined. She looked about the room and wished she had laid out her clothes. Goodness, it was only late August but it was cold. Who could have suspected it would be this cold early in the morning? Of course, she had not taken the ocean into consideration. It was always damper and colder by the ocean.

Still in bed, Sara looked around the room until she had found all her garments. Then she sprang from the bed and hurriedly pulled on her bloomers, vest and underskirts. Next she put on her long stockings. Last, she pulled on her dress and apron. She rummaged through her bag for her shawl, thinking she would only need it until the sun was high in the sky and had warmed the air.

Now dressed, Sara opened the door of her room ever so carefully so the door wouldn't squeak. Shoes in hand, Sara tiptoed down the semi-dark corridor and then down the winding staircase. As she passed through the dark kitchen, she paused only to take a small cup from the dish rack. She eased open the back door, slipped on her shoes and ran gingerly through the dewy grass towards the orchard.

Halfway to the beckoning trees of the orchard, Sara stopped, having spied some wild red berries. She examined them carefully, but passed them up because she didn't know what kind they were. Then she saw, growing close to the ground on the side of the hill, tiny clusters of wild blueberries. Quickly she filled her cup, and her mouth, then continued up the hill towards the orchard.

The cherry trees were barren and most of the apples were not yet ripe, but she found two pears and she stuffed those in the pockets of her apron for later. Then she left the orchard and headed for the King family plot. It took her only a few moments to find her mother's grave.

Looking about, she quickly gathered a bouquet of wildflowers, then arranged them on the damp grass in front of her mother's gravestone. She bent down and read the words etched in the granite.

Ruth King Stanley
1871-1893
Beloved Daughter of Abraham King,
Wife of Blair Stanley and Mother of Sara.
She loved this fair island in life and in death
They shall not be separated.

As Sara read the inscription, tears formed in her eyes. The sun was coming up now and the sky over the shimmering sea was bright pink. Birds had begun to sing and the grass smelled sweet in the early morning dampness. "Oh, Mama, I know how you could love this place," Sara said aloud. She could hear the quiver in her own voice, but she wiped her tears away and bit her lip. Then she sighed and thought of wicked Aunt Hetty. "But how *did* you get along with your own family?" she asked. Then, feeling someone's eyes on her, she turned around abruptly.

Peter Craig, Aunt Hetty's hired hand, stood only a few feet away. He smiled at her sheepishly, and Sara could see he was embarrassed. "Good morning," she managed.

Peter grinned and then shook his head. "I thought you were Felicity King, but then I didn't really think she'd be here kneelin' in the dirt. 'Specially so early in the morning. Felicity likes to sleep till the sun is high in the sky."

"This is my mother's grave," Sara said.

Peter nodded his head. "It's the King family plot. I wish I had a fancy private graveyard. My family's always been buried just anywhere they happen to die." Peter paused, and scratched his head. "You know, your Aunt Olivia seems pretty unhappy these days."

Sara pressed her lips together. "Well she won't be unhappy long because I'll be leaving quite soon."

"You haven't had any letters from home yet...course you haven't been here long."

"How do you know about what letters I have or have not received?"

Peter laughed an easy, natural laugh. "Everyone knows everything about everyone here in Avonlea."

Sara didn't answer. She just looked at Peter Craig who, she decided, was probably fourteen or thereabouts. He was tall and slim, and tanned from the summer sun.

"You'll like this place once you get used to it."

"I don't want to get used to it. I want to go home."

"Well maybe, just maybe, if you gave it a chance....Do you want me to show you around? You might as well know where you're going since you're gonna be here for a while. C'mon, hey, I'll race you to the pond." He grinned again, this time a challenging grin. "Unless you city folk can't run..."

Sara watched for a second as Peter took off towards the pond. Then, wanting to show him she could indeed run, she took off after him.

What a wonderful feeling! The wind caressed her cheeks and she could feel the dew-dampened grass squish beneath her feet. At the pond she stopped.

"It's so quiet." Sara stared into the placid water. She could see her image quite clearly. Her long, blond hair was tied back with a blue ribbon and her cheeks were flushed from running.

"It's quiet now." Peter perched on a rock. "It isn't so quiet on a spring evening when all the frogs are peeping."

Sara tilted her head. "Peeping? I thought frogs croaked."

"Bullfrogs, maybe...but here we have little tiny frogs. They're called peepers. There are thousands of them and they all peep at once."

"I'm afraid I won't be here in the spring to hear them."

Peter touched the water with his hand. "You know, the water's still warm enough to swim in— 'course so is the ocean."

"The ocean? I always heard it was very cold this far north."

"Not here. Somethin' about currents, the Gulf Stream, I think. Anyway, it stays warm till September, 'specially if the water's shallow, like in a bay."

"Well, I do like the pond. Wouldn't it be perfect if there were two matched swans?" Sara looked dreamily at the water.

Peter made a face. "Naw, swans are meaner than geese and I've got enough trouble feeding the geese."

Sara ignored his all too practical rejection of her romantic notion. "Are you going to show me the seashore too?" Sara stood up, ready to explore more of the island.

"Sure, c'mon."

"Perhaps we can find some seashells."

"Maybe. You know what? I've got a seashell, a big one. You can hold it to your ear and hear the ocean roar."

"Really?"

"Yeah, I'll show you sometime. Well, c'mon, it's a ways down to the shore."

Sara picked up her shawl and followed Peter. They ran across the fields and the sloping hill that led down to the sand dunes, and ultimately they reached the sand beach, where the waves broke gently on the shore. Perhaps, Sara thought, it was good to have one friend in Avonlea...even if she wasn't staying.

Chapter Nine

The wood stove in the kitchen burned slowly, and inside its oven a large chicken browned to golden perfection. Next to the chicken a ring of huge Prince Edward Island baking potatoes sizzled in their scrubbed jackets.

Aunt Hetty, dressed as usual in her dark tailored skirt, spotless white blouse and clean starched apron, shelled peas from the garden. Each round, hard pea hit the bottom of the big iron pot with a resounding "ping."

Olivia stood by the stove stirring the gravy round and round so that lumps wouldn't form and it wouldn't stick to the bottom of the pan as it grew thicker and richer.

"You're going to stir that gravy to death," Hetty observed with annoyance, her words emphasized by a chorus of peas "pinging" on cast iron.

"I'm upset. Hetty, I think there are other ways to deal with this situation. I'm afraid that poor Sara is starving herself to death. She's as thin as an iron railing."

"I *am* a teacher and I *do* know how to deal with children, Olivia. I wouldn't have any control in my classroom if I didn't make rules and enforce them. If you don't let them know who's boss right off the bat, they'll run all over you."

Olivia stopped stirring. "This is not just *any* child, Hetty. This is Ruth's daughter."

"Yes, precisely. Consider the facts, Olivia. First Blair Stanley ruined Ruth's life, and now he's unable to care for their child. He's sent her to us, and in so doing has cast her out as if she were a pebble on the beach! Well, we couldn't help Ruth, Olivia, but we can help Sara. We can repair the damage he's done."

Olivia didn't answer Hetty. She knew her sister well enough not to argue. Hetty wasn't entirely made of stone, and Olivia knew that Hetty, whatever she was planning, certainly had Sara's best interests at heart.

Hetty finished the last of the peas and went to the sink pump to rinse her hands. Looking out the window, she saw Sara and Peter come running up the driveway. "Here comes Sara now," Hetty announced. "Her face is red from running. That means she's had a good bit of exercise, so I imagine she's about ready to eat."

"I hope so," Olivia said softly. "I really don't want her to get sick."

The back door opened and Sara came in. She smiled at Olivia but turned away from Hetty.

"So you've decided to grace us with your presence! I suppose you're hungry, aren't you?" Hetty raised one eyebrow and looked smugly at Sara.

"Not in the slightest," Sara lied. The chicken smelled delectable, and her mouth watered at the thought of potatoes with hot chicken gravy, warm rolls, peas and milk. But she pressed her lips together and willed herself not to give in to the aroma of supper, nor the hunger she still felt in spite of the blueberries and pears she had eaten.

"You haven't eaten enough in the past two days to keep a bird alive," Olivia fretted.

Sara passed them both and headed into the hall. Hetty followed her, and she could hear

Olivia's footsteps close behind.

"You *are* going to speak to me now!" Hetty ordered. "Because I have some questions to ask you." She caught up with Sara and guided her into the sitting room. "There, you sit right there."

Sara sat in the middle of the sofa while Hetty perched across from her on the chair with the petit-point cushion.

Sara supposed she would have to answer, but she vowed she would do so in as few words as possible. She wouldn't look at Hetty, either. She picked up a book and pretended to read it.

Hetty leaned over and snatched the book, slamming it closed. "I expect your undivided attention, young lady."

Sara still refused to look at Hetty, but she glanced at Aunt Olivia who hovered in the doorway, looking distressed. Then Sara dropped her eyes and stared at the tips of her shoes.

"No, you don't have to look at me," Hetty said in irritation. "I know you are listening." Hetty took a deep breath. "Now, Sara Stanley, it is obvious to me that you have not had a proper upbringing, and that my work is cut out for me. Like it or not, you *are* going to stay here in Avonlea, and like it or not, it is never too late to begin learning. First, you will not live a life of wanton luxury under this roof! You will have chores."

Sara looked up and frowned. "Chores?"

"Yes, chores. First, you will do the dishes each night—whether or not you eat. Second, you will keep your own room neat and tidy. You can begin by properly unpacking and hanging up your clothes. Third, you will have certain chores on the farm. There are eggs to collect, berries and apples to pick, herbs to gather, and sometimes you may have to do some milking. This, I warn you, is our busiest time of year. There isn't much time left before it gets cold. We're still canning, preserving, salting and drying. There's plenty to keep your idle hands out of trouble."

Sara fairly glowered at her aunt. "I won't be staying, and I have no intention of letting you tell me what to do."

"We'll see," Hetty said, letting Sara's challenge drop. "Now, what level are you at in school?"

"I don't go to school," Sara responded somewhat arrogantly.

"That's preposterous!" Aunt Hetty stammered. "All children go to school!"

"I don't, because Papa doesn't approve of a traditional education," Sara announced.

Hetty tilted her head. "You mean to tell me there isn't a scrap of knowledge in that head of yours?"

"I didn't say that," Sara answered sharply. "I have had tutors."

"Tutors? My, aren't we the grand lady! And what in heaven's name did they tutor you in?"

"English literature, art history, painting, music and dance."

"My stars! What about mathematics and geography?" Hetty asked, still struggling with the reality of Sara's obviously privileged life.

"Papa says that traveling is the best way to study geography. I've been halfway around the world. I've even been down the Nile and I've seen the pyramids."

"How very fortunate. Unfortunately the pyramids are not on the curriculum, though the shape of their base might come up in geometry."

"Curriculum?" Sara questioned. What on earth was a curriculum?

"So, you have no knowledge of the basic curriculum?"

"I might, if I knew what it was."

Hetty folded her arms in front of her with satisfaction. She looked at Olivia hard, then returned her attention to Sara. "A curriculum is the sum total of the subjects taught at school. The basic curriculum includes reading, penmanship, math, history and geography. Naturally, the older children study advanced mathematics—algebra and geometry—as well as Latin."

"I won't be here long enough to be bothered with school," Sara said defensively.

"Oh, I think you will. School starts in just a few weeks. And just because I happen to be your aunt, there will be no favoritism. I can tell you that!"

Sara scowled. "And just because I'm your niece doesn't mean you can make me like it here!"

"No matter." Hetty stood up and smoothed out her skirt.

Olivia waited as Hetty brushed by her into the hall. Then she went straight to Sara and sat down next to her on the sofa. "Sara, dear, please come and eat. You're causing me a great deal of worry."

Sara felt her own eyes filling again with tears as she looked into her aunt's truly concerned face. Then she nodded slowly, and blinking the tears away, whispered, "I can't hurt you, Aunt Olivia. I'll eat with her, but I won't talk to her unless I absolutely have to talk to her."

Olivia hugged Sara tightly and then, pulling

"Hello," Sara smiled, trying to appear warm and friendly, as she was certain her Papa would want.

"It's spooky," Andrew said to Sara, as they hesitated at the edge of the clearing.

"Don't even look at them," Sara said, pulling herself out of the warm, sticky manure.

away, smiled. "Come along, Sara. Things will get better, I promise you."

Chapter Ten

The first day of each new school year was always marked by a kind of competition. The boys all came scrubbed cleaner than new fallen snow and sporting recent haircuts. Each one carried an apple for the teacher, and each one strived to have the biggest, reddest, juiciest apple in the orchard. The girls competed to be the best dressed and groomed. Every girl put on her very best dress and wore her biggest and best ribbons. Except Clemmie Ray. Clemmie Ray's mother was too strict to let Clemmie dress up. Janet King always said, "Clemmie's mother is so strict that her blood runs blue from pinching herself." Or, "Clemmie Ray's mother is so strict she makes Aunt Hetty look like a libertarian."

Felicity King took the first day of school very seriously. She was, in her own humble opinion, always the best dressed. And why not? She spent weeks getting ready.

As she headed towards school Felicity tossed her head just to feel her hair caress her neck. Last night she'd done her long hair up in rags and now she had fifteen perfect corkscrew curls, all gathered up in an immense yellow bow. Her dress was yellow too, with big, deep ruffles. Over her dress she wore her new white apron. It too had little ruffles over the shoulders and all along its border.

Felicity walked into the schoolroom and looked about. It hadn't changed one bit since last year. It never changed. Then she sniffed and decided that not even the smell had changed. It still smelled of chalk dust and of old boots that had been dried on the heater.

It was a long room with rows of desks. Each desk was attached to the desk before it. And each desk opened to reveal a roomy storage area which held a slate, chalk, an eraser, a proper wooden pen with a metal nib and a tiny jar of ink. There was also one book, a *Franklin Reader*. Soon each of them would have one other book, a spanking new composition book with a stiff cover that was printed to look like black marble. Aunt Hetty wouldn't pass them out right away, and when she did, they had to be cared for properly because they were used only for very special assignments.

In the exact center of the front of the room was

Aunt Hetty's desk. It had a big, green blotter in the middle and a vase in one corner. Between two bookends were four big books, and behind the desk was a large chalkboard.

Felicity turned around at the sound of others coming into the schoolroom.

"You're early," Clemmie Ray said in what Felicity always thought was a mouse-like voice. Clemmie Ray was a little older than Felicity's sister, Cecily, but more of a baby. Clemmie Ray was as plain as vanilla pudding and plump, too. Felicity thought she was a crybaby as well. But then, Felicity thought more charitably, who wouldn't cry if they had Clemmie's mother? She was not only strict, but the prissiest woman in all of Avonlea. "You must have run all the way," Felix said as he popped into the room. "I know, you just wanted to get here before Sara."

"Did not. I don't care about Miss Sara Stanley," Felicity answered sharply.

"Do so," Felix retorted, and he stuck out his tongue for good measure.

"Flies will get in your mouth and fly up and eat your brain...at least they would if you had a brain," Felicity said haughtily.

"Shut your mouth," Felix said sullenly.

"Shut yours, it's closer," Felicity returned.

Andrew strode through the door and then stood awkwardly at the back of the room. He felt bigger than anyone. Previously he had attended graded boys' schools, so most of the other students were his size. But this was a one-room school. All the students were different ages and sizes—mostly younger and smaller. Soon others flooded into the room. Some of them sat right down; others, especially the girls who wanted to be seen, milled about.

Sara appeared last. Felicity decided immediately that Sara had been waiting in the grove of trees near the school for everyone else to arrive, so that she could make an *entrance.*

Although Sara's self-control allowed her to keep her composure, she was not enjoying the eager attention of her new schoolmates, as Felicity supposed. Sara looked around and felt as if everyone were staring at her. It seemed clear no one liked her, but she held her head high and quickly slipped into a seat, wishing she could be invisible.

Felicity flounced up. "That's *my* desk, do you mind?"

"I'm sorry," Sara said, sliding out from behind the desk and standing up. She looked around for an empty place.

"This seat next to mine is empty," Cecily called out.

Sara sat down, smoothing her dress out and trying to ignore the comments of the others, but behind her she heard one girl whisper, "I heard her father's rich!" and another girl leaned over and asked Felicity, "My Ma said all her clothes come from Paris. Is that true, Felicity?" Felicity's face hardened and she replied in a voice Sara could quite clearly hear, "I wouldn't know, I'm sure. She is a distant relative and no concern of mine."

Sara considered replying, but just then Aunt Hetty swept into the room, a long pointer in hand. She tapped it loudly on the corner of her desk. "Quiet! Absolute quiet!" she demanded. Then, closing her eyes, she listened, waiting till it seemed as if everyone were holding their breath. Then she opened her eyes and scanned the students, settling on her young nephew. "Felix King, you will lead us in the Lord's Prayer."

Felix cleared his throat and began the prayer. "Our Father who art in Heaven, harrowed be Thy name..."

There was a twitter round the room, but no one interrupted him. When he had finished he opened his eyes to see that Hetty was scowling at him.

"I know that, since you were too young last year, this is the first time you've led the class in the morning prayer, but I really did think you knew it. Felix, it is not *harrowed* be Thy name, it is *hallowed* be Thy name."

"Hallowed," Felix muttered. "I don't know what that means."

"But you know what Hallowe'en is, don't you?"

"Sure, it's when we get sweets."

Everyone twittered again, but Hetty hit her pointer hard on the desk and there was instant silence. "It means sacred. I suppose you know what sacred means?"

Felix nodded his head rapidly and secretly prayed he wouldn't have to actually explain it. Hetty did not pursue it. "All rise!" she commanded imperiously. "Front and center, Felicity King!"

Felicity got up and came to the front of the room.

"You will lead us in 'God Save the King,' Felicity. Stand up straight now. Backs straight!" Hetty walked about and swiftly swatted Andrew across the seat of his pants with her pointer. "As if you're at attention! Lazy bodies make for lazy minds. Posture is a sign of proper deportment." When they were all standing like tin soldiers in a row, she commanded Felicity: "Begin!"

When they were finished and had sat down again, Hetty smiled. "Class, I would like you to say hello to Sara Stanley and Andrew King. They are new to Avonlea, and I hope you will make them feel welcome and at home for the school year. Now Sara, can you recite the two-times table for me?"

Sara stared at Hetty and felt her cheeks go hot as the rest of the class stared at her and then began to giggle. What, she wondered, was a times table?

"Well, Sara, don't stare at me as if you've lost your senses."

"I don't know what you mean," Sara answered honestly.

Hetty let out her breath and shook her head. "Well, then I suppose you will have to sit with the younger children till you *do* know what I mean."

Sara started to gather up her books. "If that's what you wish," she answered, feeling stubborn.

Hetty's face looked like a thundercloud. "Not only will you sit with the Level One children, but you will stay after school and practice your times tables until you *do* know them!"

Sara tossed her head defiantly as she got up and changed seats.

Hetty didn't even look at her. "Andrew King! Will you recite the twelve-times table beginning with twelve times six?"

Andrew stood up as straight as he could. His face was beet-red, but he began, "Twelve times six is seventy-two, twelve times seven is eighty-four, twelve times eight is ninety-six, twelve times nine is one hundred and eight, twelve times ten is one hundred and twenty, twelve times eleven is one hundred and thirty-two, and twelve times twelve is one hundred and forty-four."

Hetty looked down her long nose at him. "That's very good, Andrew."

Sara shifted uncomfortably in her chair. Times tables appeared to be nothing more than multiplied sums. Well, she thought, I won't be after school too long.

Chapter Eleven

It was nearly five o'clock. The warm, friendly kitchen of Rose Cottage smelled of Olivia's freshly baked blueberry pie. On the stove, a slow-cooking stew simmered in its own rich, thick gravy while loaves of home-baked bread and a platter of dinner rolls cooled on the counter.

Olivia bustled about the kitchen preparing dinner, but her mind was truly elsewhere. She wondered how her niece was adjusting to school, to Avonlea, to the other children, and most of all to Hetty, whose bark, Olivia well knew, was worse than her bite.

"No matter," Olivia murmured to herself, stirring her stew. "I can't do much to make things easier for Sara except love her and see to it that she eats well."

No sooner had Hetty entered her mind than the back door opened and in she bustled, books under her arm.

Olivia looked up and smiled. "Well, how did your day go?"

"It went as I expected," Hetty answered crisply.

Olivia had hoped Hetty would be more forthcoming, but she should have known better. Hetty only responded to direct questions. "How was Sara's first day?"

Hetty shook her head. "Well, it's as clear as clear can be that her education has huge gaps in it"—she paused, and the smallest of smiles curved around her thin lips—"but I will say she's a clever little thing. She didn't seem to know her times tables so I kept her after school. With almost no instruction she produced them soon enough. Yes, no doubt about it. She learns quickly."

Olivia smiled broadly. "Oh, I felt she was clever, Hetty. I felt it the minute I looked at her. She has bright eyes, bright interested eyes."

"A schoolteacher has to base her assessments on more than just 'a feeling' and bright eyes, Olivia. Performance is what counts. After all, chickens have bright eyes."

Olivia suppressed a smile. "I'm sure you only base your assessments on performance, Hetty. I know you would never let affection color your opinion."

Hetty looked at Olivia skeptically. "Are you mocking me?"

Olivia opened her eyes wide with innocence. "Of course not. I just meant, I know how seriously you take your teaching."

"I'd be cheating the children if I didn't take it seriously. It's a terrible responsibility, teaching. At any rate, it's a profound relief for me to discover that Sara isn't *all* Stanley. And she isn't one who bends any way the wind blows either. Ruth was like that, she was like a willow in the wind."

Hetty sat down, and her eyes took on a familiar, faraway look. It was a look she got whenever she talked about Ruth. "Remember, Olivia...

remember when Ruth wanted to be an actress? She used to dress up and act out all sorts of plays...and she'd make up stories, too. Then, poof! All desire to be an actress was gone and she wanted to be an artist."

"I remember, she used to sit down by the sea and paint."

Hetty shook her head as if to dispel thoughts of her dead sister. "And then, poof! Blair Stanley appeared and she gave up everything for him. Everything. A willow in the wind...that's the way she was."

Olivia nodded, then said in a low voice, "I think Sara has Ruth's spirit, though."

Hetty nodded her agreement. "Yes, I caught her looking at me today, and when I looked up it was just like looking into Ruth's eyes. It gave me quite a start, I can tell you. It was like traveling back through time."

Hetty pressed her lips together and turned away. Olivia knew she was feeling strong emotions.

Hetty recovered quickly, however, and began putting the rolls in a basket. "Best to cover up these rolls, Olivia. If they're covered and kept on the stove top they'll stay warm till dinner."

"I'm glad you can see how clever Sara is,"

Olivia said, ignoring her sister's attempt to change the subject.

"Yes, Sara's clever and she's bold," Hetty allowed. "But she's not forward. She knows when to keep her own counsel and she certainly has a generous helping of the King pride."

Olivia did smile this time. "It sounds like King pride talking right now, Hetty."

Hetty tossed her head. "Humph!" she declared, clearly not wanting to admit to her own generous share of that emotion. "Where is Sara, anyway? I certainly hope she's upstairs, working on her times tables."

Olivia laughed. "Oh, Sara's not home. I thought you knew where she was."

"Not home? She left me more than an hour ago."

"No need to worry, Hetty. Sara's probably playing with her cousins."

Hetty looked annoyed. "Without telling us where she is? Isn't that just like a Stanley? Running off! Well, this house has rules, and those rules are going to be laid down when she comes home!"

Olivia shook her head. "Children are children, Hetty. I'm sure she's having a lovely time. It's good to see that she's starting to fit in, to make friends. It's a great relief to me, I can tell you."

"As long as she's not late for dinner," Hetty said.

The sun was beginning to drop behind the knoll, and it seemed to Sara as if the sky were all pink, blue and gold. Great white gulls played tag over the water, while on a nearby rock a dark cormorant perched, its scalloped wings outstretched, stock-still, waiting for its prey in the calm water of the inlet.

Sara watched the sea for a long moment. Then she finished collecting her wildflowers and went directly to her mother's grave. She kneeled and, carefully removing the flowers she had left before, replaced them with fresh blossoms of wild purple aster and feathery goldenrod. These were the last wildflowers of summer. Soon, only the bright red cranberries, foxberries and holly berries would give color to those plants that didn't sleep in winter. "When there aren't any more flowers," Sara promised, "I'll bring berries."

When she had finished arranging her wildflowers, Sara spread out her shawl and sat down on it, opposite her mother's grave. "I like your island more and more," she admitted in a near-whisper. "And Aunt Olivia is very kind." She frowned. "Still, it's going to be lonely, Mama. I don't think many of the children like me. I don't think they like Andrew much, either. We're both outcasts because we're 'from away,' as everyone keeps saying." Sara sighed. "I do wish Papa would write. And I do miss Nanny Louisa." Then, even more softly she whispered, "Things aren't the way I thought they'd be." Her voice quivered, but she did not cry. She had cried herself out.

"Sara?"

She turned suddenly to see Andrew standing quietly a few feet away. He carried his books in a book-strap, and he was wearing his cap, which was perpetually cocked to one side. "What are you doing here?" she asked.

"I came looking for you."

"Oh," Sara replied. She was surprised, but not at all unhappy to see him. In some ways Andrew was worse off than she. She had to bear only Aunt Hetty's sharp tongue, but poor Andrew lived with Alec and Janet King. She had a room of her own at Rose Cottage, but Andrew had to share a room with that awful little Felix King and, even worse, he had to live under the same roof with Felicity.

"How are you?" Andrew asked with concern.

"Aunt Janet said you almost starved yourself."

Sara looked down at the grass, then she nodded. "I'm eating now," she admitted.

"I also heard about your father. I'm sorry."

Sara pressed her lips together and, looking up, narrowed her eyes. "Don't you dare say anything about my father! Whatever you heard about him is a pack of lies! Understand?"

Andrew looked embarrassed, and he shifted his weight from one foot to the other. "Sure, I understand. Come on, walk with me. It's almost dinnertime, you know. I don't know about you, but Aunt Janet doesn't take it well if I'm late."

Sara laughed. "Aunt Hetty doesn't take anything well."

"Will you walk home from school with me tomorrow?" Andrew asked suddenly.

Sara half smiled and nodded. "If you're sure you want to be seen with me."

Andrew smiled. "Race you down the hill?"

Sara wasn't going to let Andrew get a head start as she had let Peter do the other day. "Last one to the bottom is a rotten egg," she called out, taking off as fast as she could run.

Chapter Twelve

"Stand closer together," Felicity commanded Cecily and Clemmie Ray. "You're both so short that you turn the rope too low," she complained.

They were all in the school yard. Felix sat on a nearby rock, watching with distaste as the three girls skipped rope. He wanted to play marbles, but the other boys had gone.

Felicity darted into the turning rope. "The King of France went up the hill, with forty thousand men," she panted as she jumped. "The King of France came down the hill, and ne'er went up again...." She darted out and Cecily and Clemmie Ray let the rope go slack.

"I haven't missed yet," Felicity reminded them.

"You never miss," Clemmie Ray replied sullenly. "So we never get our turn."

"I know other words to that rhyme," Felix put in.

"They're impolite and we don't want to hear them," Felicity said cuttingly.

"C'mon," Felix said, standing up. "It's almost time for us to do our chores. We'd better get going."

Felicity, Felix, Cecily and Clemmie Ray gathered up their books and walked slowly down the red dirt road. Cecily and Clemmie Ray were good friends and they walked slightly behind Felix and Felicity.

Felicity pulled her shawl around her shoulders and marched purposefully ahead. "I'm glad Sara had to stay after school yesterday. It served her right. She thinks she's so smart."

"That Andrew's just as bad," Felix pouted. "All he ever talks about is how much he knows. At least you don't have to share a room with Sara. I have to share a room with that Andrew. The two of them are such show-offs."

"I know. Just look at those dresses she wears to school. Who does she think she is, anyway? The Queen of England?"

Cecily looked down at her own frock. It had once been Felicity's, and it had been washed so much the color and shine had faded from the gingham. "I think her dresses are pretty," said Cecily wistfully.

Clemmie Ray, whose dress, made out of a Monarch Flour sack, was even more faded than Cecily's, was quick to agree. "So do I. I wish I could wear dresses like that. But my Ma would never let me." She didn't add, "even if we had the money to buy them."

Felicity stomped her foot on the dirt path. "I just wish Sara's father would come and get her! I wish he would come real fast."

Clemmie Ray shook her head slowly. "My Ma says there's not much hope of that. She says her father is a scandal. Whatever that means."

Felicity turned and looked down her nose at Clemmie Ray. "It means, Clemmie, that Sara's father has tarnished our family's good name. I personally am ashamed to be related to her."

Cecily looked at her sister then said quietly but firmly, "I like Sara, and I like Andrew, too. They're our cousins and you shouldn't talk that way, Felicity King."

"We shouldn't talk that way, we shouldn't talk that way. Yeah, yeah, yeah," Felicity said, mimicking her younger sister. "You're such a silly little do-gooder, Cecily. A real goody-two-shoes."

Felix grinned mischievously. "Hey, Felicity, maybe we should show Andrew and Miss Sara Stanley who's boss around here."

Felicity smiled. "And I think I know just how to do that.

"How?" Felix asked, scratching his head. Felicity was always too quick for him. Her mind seemed to work at high speed.

"The trapdoor," Felicity whispered so Cecily and Clemmie Ray wouldn't hear. "You *know* where it leads."

Felix slapped his leg and laughed. "That'll fix them," he agreed happily.

"Come on, let's get home. If I'm right, Sara and Andrew will come by just about the time we're doing our chores in the barn."

Felix smirked wickedly. "We'll have to find a way to lure them."

Felicity giggled. "I know how to do that. You just wait and see."

The low, sloping chicken coop was right out-side the barn. Felicity and Felix were gathering eggs, all the while keeping a lookout for Sara and Andrew's approach. "We'll get them, *and* we'll get our chores done," she announced.

Suddenly, with undisguised joy, Felix nudged his sister. "Here they come," he whispered.

"Little Miss La-de-da is in for a surprise," Felicity predicted.

"And Little Lord Andrew," Felix added, rel-ishing the thought of what was to come. He put down his basket of eggs and called out, "Hey, Andrew! Sara! Come here!"

Immediately, Felicity and Felix ran into the

barn and climbed up the ladder to the loft. "Up here!" Felix called out.

Felicity leaned out the loft window. "The cat has had her kittens! Do you want to come and see them? They're ever so tiny and cute."

Felix used his arm to signal. "They're up here!" He turned to his sister, "Come on, hurry up! It's time to spring our trap."

"Oh, I've never seen newborn kittens." Sara pulled Andrew towards the barn.

Andrew followed, not telling her he thought newborn kittens looked like mice.

Sara led Andrew into the barn, which smelled of sweet hay and pungent manure. She blinked in the semi-darkness. "It's so bright outside, I'm blind in here."

"I can't see a thing either," Andrew admitted.

"Felix! Felicity! Where are you?" Sara called out.

"We're up here," Felix called out from the loft.

"Do hurry," Felicity implored. "The mother cat is taking the kittens away from the barn."

Sara and Andrew climbed the ladder to the loft, where it seemed even darker. "Felicity?" Sara called out.

"Over here," she called back sweetly.

Sara and Andrew walked through the thick

hay towards Felicity's voice.

Suddenly the floor fell out from beneath them.

Sara screamed as they both fell through the trapdoor to the mucking-out section of the barn below. They landed, waist-deep, in straw and cow manure. Sara blinked disbelievingly, as the great pink pig who wallowed in the manure twitched his fat pink nose at her.

Above them, Felix and Felicity, laughing loudly, hung their heads through the trapdoor. "Guess we got you!" Felix called out.

"You sure don't look like you've been to Paris now!" Felicity called out nastily. "And you don't smell of French perfume, either!"

Felix pulled on Felicity's sleeve. "We better get our eggs and get home," he prodded. "No telling how mad they are, and Andrew's bigger than me."

Felicity nodded, and they hurriedly climbed down and disappeared into the darkness of the barn.

"Don't even look at them," Sara said, pulling herself out of the warm, sticky manure. How could she have thought Felicity just might have been ready to offer the hand of friendship to her? It was all a trick.

"I'm going to kill them, I really am," Andrew

announced, clenching his fists.

Sara shook her head. "That's what they want."

"Then I'm going to tell Uncle Alec. That's what I'm going to do! And then they'll be in for it."

"No, that's too easy. Listen to me, Andrew. Don't let's get angry, let's get revenge."

Andrew smiled at her. "Do you have an idea?"

"Not yet. But I will. I just have to think. In the meantime, we'd better clean up. Let's go to the pond."

The two of them walked as quickly as they could to the pond. "I feel like my own smell is chasing me," Andrew said as they hurried on. He shook his head. "The water's going to be cold."

"We'll just have to bear it," Sara said. "You mustn't let them know they've succeeded in upsetting us, Andrew."

"I think you're a better actress than I am an actor."

By the edge of the pond, Sara slipped off her dress and rinsed it out. She wasn't at all cold in just her underskirts, because it had been warm all day and the warmth lingered. She hung her dress on a branch to dry. Once, she had thought it would be fun getting dirty, but this had not been fun because it wasn't a game. Felix and Felicity had taken advantage of her and Andrew: they'd been just plain mean.

Gingerly, Sara and Andrew washed in the cold pond water. "Good thing the sun's been shining all day," Andrew said. "Otherwise the water would really be like ice."

"They won't get away with it, Andrew. We'll think of some way to get them back. We'll think of the perfect way to get even."

Peter Craig suddenly poked his head through the low bushes next to the pond. "They got you, did they? Felix and Felicity, I mean? You know, you're not the first people they've played that trick on."

"On you too?" Andrew asked.

Peter blushed. "Yeah, a long time ago."

"How did you find us?" Sara asked, as she splashed water on her legs and arms.

"Followed the smell," he laughed. Then, more seriously, "I saw you running away from the barn."

"We'll get even," Sara vowed.

"If it's revenge you want, I'm sure Peg Bowen could do something to them. If anyone could, she could."

"Who is Peg Bowen?" Sara asked with curiosity. It seemed to her she'd heard the name before, but she couldn't remember where.

"They say she's a witch," Peter confided. "Everyone's afraid of her."

Sara smiled. She remembered now that she'd heard Clemmie Ray talking about the witch, Peg Bowen. "Are Felix and Felicity afraid of her?"

Peter nodded. "Oh, yes."

"Can you take us to her?" Sara asked.

"Well, actually, I have to take her these eggs...but I'm not sure how she'd feel about meeting strangers."

"Then we'll find out where she lives and go by ourselves."

"I don't think that's a very good idea," Andrew interjected.

Peter rubbed his chin. "I'll take you," he relented. "But you mustn't act afraid."

Sara looked at him hard. "I'm not afraid," she said firmly. "I don't believe in witches...well, not really."

Peter covered the eggs carefully. "This way." He led them towards the pine forest beyond the knoll.

Now Peg Bowen was a rather special person, and though some people called her a witch, that didn't mean they didn't respect her. The truth was that, like her mother before her, Peg Bowen studied the plants that grew on the island. She knew how to make medicines and ease pain. She lived a distance from Avonlea, in a small house in the pine forest, and yet she always seemed to know what was going on in the village and to the people who lived thereabouts. The children who called her a witch would have been very surprised to know that some of the most respected people in the community visited Peg Bowen for medicines.

The forest floor was covered with pinecones and needles, except where it was completely shaded. In those darkened places a strange, springy kind of moss grew. Here and there, small ponds or springs saturated the ground, and wild, strange mushrooms grew in the dampness.

"Peg Bowen knows everything," Peter told them. "I don't know all the plants hereabouts, but I know some. I know she makes a cure for red-eye out of Indian Pipe—that's that funny white plant. Looks sort of like a bunch of mushrooms hanging on a plant. Some folks call it 'corpse plant.'"

"Why?" Sara asked.

"I don't know for certain." Peter slowed his pace. "I guess it's called that 'cause it's completely white—stem, leaves, everything. Sort of like it was a dead thing—like the corpse of a green plant."

"I'm not really certain going to this Peg Bowen's is a good idea," Andrew put in. The talk of corpses—even if they were plants—was starting to make him nervous.

"Too late now," Peter said, stopping and pointing through the trees. "There's her house. And unless I miss my guess, she already knows we're here."

Peg Bowen's cottage was in the center of a small clearing. It was a ramshackle wooden affair. Flowers and herbs grew all around it and were hung outside to dry in bunches. It was much smaller than any house Sara had ever seen. Inside, it couldn't have been more than one tiny room.

"It's spooky," Andrew said as they hesitated at the edge of the clearing. "I sure am glad its daylight."

Sara frowned at him. "I do believe you've spent too long reading Grimm's Fairy Tales, Andrew King. This isn't the Black Forest and we're not Hansel and Gretel."

"I'm not poking my head in her oven anyway," Andrew said.

Peter strode across the clearing towards the cottage, followed quickly by Sara and Andrew. Sara felt completely intrigued, as if the house were calling out to her, as if soon all its mysteries would be revealed.

Just before they got to the door, it opened, and an old woman stepped out.

Sara stared at her. She was dressed in layers of clothing, her hair was frizzy and her leathery face was a network of deep wrinkles. Her eyes were sharp and appraising, and they moved quickly from one person to another.

"Hello...Peg..." Peter began.

Sara felt just a tiny bit uneasy as Peg Bowen's eyes came to rest on her.

"Well, well. I wondered when you would pay me a visit, Sara Stanley."

Sara was taken aback that this strange woman knew her name—in fact, seemed to know all about her. It was as if Peg Bowen's sharp eyes could see right through her. "How did you know who I was—?" Sara ventured.

But Peg Bowen cut her off. "Them my eggs, Peter? Chickens layin' again, I see."

Peter nodded. "Yes, the chickens are fine." He moved restlessly and then decided to come right out with it. "We want to play a trick on Felicity and Felix King. We need your help."

Peg's eyes swung back to Sara, and it was Sara to whom she seemed to be speaking. "Ah, yes.

Them King children deserve a comeuppance. They've never been much charitable to ol' Peg here...and they're not much charitable to you either," she surmised.

Sara looked back at Peg Bowen unblinkingly. "We don't really want to hurt them."

"We just want to make them feel the way we felt," Andrew added. He felt braver now.

Peg fished in her pocket and smiled. "I think your cousins should try some of my magic seeds." She leaned towards Sara. "You will see, Sara Stanley, that trickery of the mind is just as potent as trickery of deed."

"I think I know what you mean," Sara said.

"Well, you come inside and we'll have some tea. I'll tell you how my magic seeds work."

Sara nodded and started to climb the steps.

"Is your oven lit?" Andrew suddenly asked.

Peg Bowen didn't smile. "The tea is already hot, if that's what you mean."

Aunt Hetty would have been aghast to know that Sara was having tea with Peg Bowen, but at that particular moment she had no idea where Sara was.

"I told her to come straight home!" Hetty fretted. "That was hours ago. Does that child not listen? What a question. Her mother never listened either. They're like two peas in a pod."

"I'm sure she just forgot the time. There aren't so many nice days left, Hetty. Soon it will be cold outside. Let her enjoy herself. She'll be here. After all, she was a little late yesterday as well."

"I would certainly like to know where she disappears to."

Olivia smiled. "Well, I found fresh flowers on Ruth's grave. I think she may go there sometimes."

Hetty turned and looked at Olivia. Though Olivia's revelation made her feel ashamed for asking about Sara's whereabouts, she didn't show it. "Well," Hetty hesitated, "she should still be here in time for dinner." She leaned over and pulled the curtain aside so she could look out the window. "It is getting late."

Olivia suppressed a smile. "You know, if I didn't know better, I'd say you were concerned about her."

"Good grief, here she comes now!" Hetty said in irritation. "Good heavens! Where's her dress? She's running around in her undergarments!"

Sara bounded into the house, hoping not to be seen till she had washed properly.

"In the name of Providence!" Hetty shrieked.

"No, don't tell me! Maybe people in Montreal run around in all states of undress, but they do not do so in Avonlea!"

Sara paused, looking first at Hetty and then at Olivia.

"Do go to the bathroom and get yourself decent!" Hetty commanded. "Then come and help get dinner ready."

Olivia sniffed the air. Manure, she thought to herself. The pungent odor was unmistakable. She smiled at Sara and grasped her shoulder firmly. "Let's go to the bathroom," she said as soon as they were out of earshot. "My goodness, Sara. Whatever happened? I do think a bath is in order, not just a wash. I'll get the tub."

"I guess I do need a bath."

Olivia smiled. "I'm sure there's a story here. But I'll wait for you to tell me."

Sara nodded. "There is, and I will tell you. But not for a few days...not till the story has a proper ending."

Chapter Thirteen

At promptly three-thirty, Aunt Hetty rang the big bell on her desk to dismiss the class. "Don't run! Leave in an orderly fashion!" she called out. But this was the only time during the day when her words were in vain. The students hurried noisily out of class, pushing and shoving as if the schoolhouse were on fire. Hetty sighed as she looked at the empty schoolroom. Then she sat down. There were, as always, papers to grade before going home.

Outside, the class quickly dispersed. Some of the girls went to play at skipping rope, some of the boys ran to play tag. Still others began walking slowly towards home.

"Now remember," Sara said as soon as she and Andrew were a few feet from the schoolroom door, and well out of Aunt Hetty's hearing range, "this won't work unless they think *they're* fooling *us.*"

"I'm not as good at this sort of thing as you are," Andrew protested.

"I'm certain you'll do fine. Now be sure Felicity and Felix see our every move. As soon as we're closer to them, you come close and show me the seeds."

Andrew nodded, wondering if this well-laid plan would work.

"Here, now," Sara whispered as she saw Felix and Felicity walking behind them.

Andrew took the little packet of seeds out of

his pocket and Sara stood close to him. They whispered together until Felix came bounding up, with Felicity close behind.

"What'cha got there?" Felix asked, leaning over, his face practically twitching with curiosity.

Andrew quickly covered the packet in his hand. "Nothing."

"I saw you. You were looking at something. What was it?" Felicity demanded.

Sara grabbed Andrew's arm. "Come on, Andrew. Let's go." She suppressed her delight when Andrew, just as planned, dropped the packet of seeds to the ground and a few fell out.

"What's that?" Felix asked as he bent down.

Andrew quickly bent over and covered the seeds with his hand. "Do you think we'd tell you?" he replied briskly.

"You think you're so smart." Felix kicked the dirt with the toe of his worn shoe.

Andrew looked up, ready to meet the challenge. "Do you know why I'm so smart?"

Sara tugged on Andrew's arm harder. "Do be quiet. Don't tell them anything. It's our secret."

"Why?" Felicity asked, her brow creased with a frown.

Andrew opened his hands to reveal the package of magic seeds. "Because of these," he told her.

Sara stomped her foot in mock outrage. "Oh, Andrew! I knew you couldn't keep a secret!"

"What's that stuff?" Felicity asked, bending over as if she were going to sniff it.

Andrew attempted to make his voice sound as mysterious as possible. "Magic seeds."

"I don't believe you. They look like ordinary cucumber seeds to me."

Sara stepped between Andrew and Felicity. "That's what they are, Felicity. Just ordinary cucumber seeds. It's very clever of you to realize that. There's no way we could fool you."

Andrew feigned irritation and refused to budge, even when Sara pulled on him. "Peg Bowen gave them to me the first day I arrived. She was at the station. She told me how to use them. You eat one and make a wish—any wish— and it comes true."

"Andrew!" Sara said, pulling on him. "Don't tell them another thing!"

"Peg Bowen?" Felicity's eyes grew wide. "Avonlea's Peg Bowen? The one who lives in the woods?"

"The witch!" Felix said, almost reverently.

"I don't believe you." Felicity said, though not with absolute certainty.

"Fine." Sara heaved a deep sigh. "Fine. Andrew,

will you come along. You've said quite enough. After all, the seeds were given to *you*."

"All I know," Andrew said, now feeling more confident in this, his first acting role, "is that I never was smart enough to recite my twelve-times table before I took this stuff. And you remember Sara's first day of school? She didn't even know what a times table was! But she sure knew them the next day. I'd never heard of such a thing as magic seeds in my life, but they're magic all right."

"Then let me have one. I'll try it. Better yet, let Felix have one. He needs to be smart more than anyone."

Andrew shook his head. "Mind you, you can't just take it any old way. You have to follow the directions."

"What directions?" Felicity asked, looking suspicious.

"You have to take the seed on a Friday night at exactly midnight...in a church graveyard when the moon is full."

Felicity screwed up her face. "That's disgusting."

Felix was still wide-eyed. "Why do you have to take it in the graveyard?" he pressed.

Andrew returned to his mysterious tone.

"Because, Peg Bowen said that you need the left-over life force from the dead human bones!"

Felicity lifted her head high. "You wouldn't catch me believing all that hocus pocus."

"Me neither," Felix said, again kicking the dirt. Then, under his breath, "Sure wish there were such a thing."

Andrew stuffed the seed package into his pocket. He shrugged and opened his hands expressively. "Fine, fine. I'm sorry I even told you about it."

Sara again pulled on him and this time Andrew followed. "I told you, Andrew! Now they'll probably tattle to their parents," she said in a loud voice. "You can tell they're tattletales."

"We are not," Felix called out sullenly. Secretly, he was thinking about the magic seeds and how they could change everything. He would wish...he would wish to be smart, of course. But he would also wish to get the best of Felicity, to have a new pretty, sweet schoolteacher who wouldn't ever give him any homework, and he'd wish he didn't have to do more chores, that he could be rich, that he could just go into the store and have all the candy he wanted....

"Felix!" Felicity snapped. "What are you doing?"

"Just thinking."

Felicity had been thinking, too. How wonderful it would be to have anything one wished for....She turned suddenly and ran up and grabbed Andrew's arm. "I'm sorry! Wait, I didn't mean it. Do you think I could have some?" She blinked into Andrew's eyes and smiled sweetly.

She's flirting, Sara thought with satisfaction. For Felicity to be so nice could only mean she really wanted the seeds, that she intended to use them.

"Please?" Felicity begged.

"Oh, all right," Andrew relented. "But remember, you have to take it on a Friday night at midnight in the graveyard." Carefully, he measured out some seeds for Felicity and Felix.

"If they're really magic," Felicity said with bravado, "they'll work without following your silly directions. You won't catch *me* in any graveyard."

"Me neither," Felix added.

Andrew again turned. "Suit yourselves," he said, hurrying to catch up with Sara. "I told you how to use them. If you don't use them right, you'll just waste them."

Sara and Andrew walked on for a while, not

daring to look back or say a word to each other. Then Andrew, unable to stand it a second longer, looked behind. "They're gone," he said, grinning from ear to ear. Sara turned to face him. They shook hands heartily and then both dissolved into laughter.

When they got to the road that led to Rose Cottage, they parted company. "I can hardly wait till Friday," Sara said, smiling.

"Me too," Andrew agreed.

Sara skipped the rest of the way to Rose Cottage. She had actually laughed and she was having fun. Of course Felicity and Felix would be angry, but they had started it, and once she and Andrew had evened the score...then perhaps things could be different.

At dinner a half hour later, Sara looked intently into her soup while contemplating the sweet revenge she and Andrew would have on Felicity and Felix. Remembering her vow, Sara did not speak to Aunt Hetty, and because of her silence, no one talked very much.

At this particular moment, Peter, who usually ate with them, was loudly slurping his soup. Every now and again he would kick Sara under the table and grin.

Hetty looked from one of them to the other in

annoyance. They were trying to bother her, she decided. "Don't slurp your soup, Peter, or you will find yourself eating in the chicken coop." She put her napkin on the table and looked harshly at him.

Olivia moved uneasily. Then, unable to stand the silence a minute longer, she turned to Sara. "Tell me about school today. Did you see Felicity?"

"Yes," Sara replied, not wanting to begin a conversation that might come to involve Hetty.

"I do hope you two will be great friends...once you get to know each other. And I must get to know Andrew better. It's difficult to know him as well as I know you, of course, because he lives at the farm while you live here. Janet says he's a very serious boy, but then that shouldn't surprise anyone. His father was serious, too. You know, Sara, Andrew's father and your mother were born exactly a year apart. They were born on the same day of the same month...and they were complete opposites...just like night and day, Mother always said..."

Hetty shook her head at Olivia. "Don't prattle on so! If you ate as fast as you talk, you'd be finished with your soup like the rest of us."

Olivia jumped up. "Oh, dear, excuse me. I didn't mean to keep anyone waiting. I'll collect the dishes." The fact was, she could hardly wait to escape.

Hetty looked at Sara. "Make yourself useful," she suggested firmly. "Help your Aunt Olivia clear the table."

Sara stood up and began clearing the dishes from the table. But she realized too late that the soup bowls and saucers were not piled correctly, and she nearly dropped them as she put them on the sideboard.

"Please do be careful," Hetty said. "Great-Grandmother Elizabeth's china has managed to stay in the family for three generations. I would hate to see your carelessness put an end to its immortality. Now could you please bring the roast to the table?"

Sara lifted the heavy platter off the sideboard.

Olivia bit her lower lip. "Oh, Hetty, I'm sure the platter is much too heavy for her. Here, let me help you Sara."

"Sara is perfectly capable. It has been my experience that children only learn by doing."

The platter was heavy. Not only was the roast very large, but it was surrounded by vegetables and potatoes.

"Yes, it's high time Sara learned that to be waited on in life is the exception not the—"

"Oh!" Sara screamed. She had just started to lower the heavy platter to the table when the roast slipped right off and into Hetty's lap. Worse yet, the platter slipped right out of her hand. It crashed to the floor and broke into a hundred pieces.

"—rule." Hetty finished her sentence and stared at the dinner in her lap.

"Oh!" Sara felt for a moment as if she herself might fall over. Her face went ashen. Then she turned and ran up the stairs, tears already streaming from her eyes. She hadn't meant to drop the roast, or break Great-Grandmother's platter.

She ran into her room and the door swung shut behind her. She flung herself on the bed, crying. "I can't do anything right!" she said aloud. "Nothing." She sniffed and tried to stop crying, but the tears wouldn't stop. Nobody here in Avonlea—except maybe Aunt Olivia—really wanted her. She was a bother, a "responsibility and an obligation." And now she had broken an important family heirloom.

She pulled herself off the bed and went to the desk. Once she'd found a piece of paper and a pen, she began writing. It wasn't the first letter she had written her father, but it was the most desperate.

"Dear Papa,

"Please, please, please come and get me and take me home...."

Sara turned abruptly at the sound of her bedroom door opening. Hetty was standing there, still wiping the gravy off her skirt with a cloth.

Hetty's lips were pressed tight, but Sara couldn't help noticing that she looked more concerned than angry. "There's no use crying over spilled milk, child."

Sara's tears flowed harder than ever. "I'm sorry. I'm sorry. I really didn't mean to break Great-Grandmother's platter. It was an accident."

Hetty looked at her young niece. So like her mother, she thought. Instinctively, she wanted to hold Sara, to tell her everything would be all right...to tell her she loved her. But she couldn't. All her life Hetty King had fought displays of emotion. She couldn't bring herself to break the pattern now.

Sara looked into Hetty's face and thought she could almost see a smile creep around Hetty's lips.

"Well, I must say I'm glad you didn't throw the roast at me on purpose," Hetty said. Then she added, "Although how you could be so clumsy is beyond me."

Sara looked into Hetty's eyes. "I've never had
to serve at the table before. The maids always did
it."

"I'm sure they did. But you won't find maids
in Avonlea. Things are different here."

"You don't have to tell me again," Sara said in
a near whisper as again tears filled her eyes. "To
you, I'm just a responsibility." She imitated the
tone she'd heard in Hetty's voice that first night
she'd argued with Nanny Louisa.

"Ah." Hetty looked as though she understood. Then she quickly said, "Don't talk such
nonsense, child."

"It's true! You said so! You told Nanny
Louisa!" Sara insisted.

For the very first time, Hetty avoided her
eyes. She sat down on the edge of the bed and
shook her head. "We were all very unprepared
that night. And sometimes one says things that
one doesn't really mean."

Sara interrupted. "I don't fit in here. You can
send me back. You don't have to fulfill your duty!"

Hetty looked up now, her voice firm. "I have
no intention of sending you anywhere. You are
going to be here for a good while, young lady, so I
suggest it's time you learned to fit in."

With that, Hetty stood up and Sara blinked at

her. Hetty took the letter off the desk and read it, then she put it down. "And writing endless letters to your father won't help in the least. I don't know why you bother, since Providence knows they may never reach him."

Sara's face flushed, and she wiped the tears from her cheek. "I don't care if they do or don't! I miss him! And I want my Nanny Louisa!"

"You're much too old to need a nursemaid."

"She wasn't a nursemaid! She was my friend. My only friend."

Hetty sat back down on the edge of the bed and looked at Sara hard, then reached out and touched her shoulder. "Sara, there's really no need for such an outburst."

Sara shook her head. "You don't understand. How could you? Haven't you ever missed someone so badly that something inside of you just seemed to shrivel up and die?"

Sara's question had hit home. Hetty looked steadily at Sara and her face softened. She blinked back her own tears. Did Sara really not know?

For a moment, Sara thought Hetty was going to cry. But Hetty looked away when she spoke. "Yes. It was like that for me when your mother died, Sara. I was fifteen years older than your mother, you know. I raised her. She was more than a sister, she was like my own child...."

Hetty suddenly jumped up and smoothed out her skirt nervously. "So," she said, attempting to cover her unusual display of emotion, "when you finish your letter—if you must finish it—come downstairs. Perhaps you could read to me. We have lots of interesting books on the parlor shelves, many of which were your mother's."

Sara suddenly realized she had stopped crying. Clearly, the person Aunt Hetty was on the outside was very different from the person she was on the inside.

Hetty had her bony hand on the doorknob when she turned, a rare smile on her face. "By the way, Great-Grandmother's platter wasn't one of my favorites."

Chapter Fourteen

Friday passed with agonizing slowness. "Do you think they'll show up?" Andrew asked as he and Sara made their way back to the King farm after school.

"I'm sure they will," Sara assured him.

Andrew smirked. "I'll listen for them, then I'll go out my window. I'll run all the way so I can get ahead of them. When I pass Rose Cottage I'll howl like a dog. Then you climb down the roof and meet me by the side of the church. We'll get to the graveyard before them. That way we can hear everything and surprise them."

"Sweet revenge," Sara smiled. "I can hardly wait."

Now, at long last, the hour of revenge was approaching. Sara stood, fully clothed, in front of her open window. She took a deep, deep breath of air as she waited for Andrew.

She thought about the last few days. Something had changed between her and Aunt Hetty the night she accidentally broke the platter. She couldn't quite put her finger on it. Aunt Hetty still ordered her about and lectured her at every opportunity. She expected a lot and, as promised, she treated her exactly as she treated the other children in school. But still....

Sara sighed. She supposed the thing that had changed was that now she knew that Aunt Hetty really cared about her, that for all her strictness, Hetty was a real person with real feelings.

Sara leaned out the window, and was midway through another deep breath of night air when she heard a soft knock on the door. She turned and jumped into her bed, clothes and all, and pulled the covers up right under her chin.

"Sara, are you in bed, dear?" Olivia's inquiring voice asked softly.

"Yes, Aunt Olivia."

"Lights out, now. Just a minute and I'll come and tuck you in."

For a moment, Olivia's footsteps retreated, but within seconds she returned, opening the door and slipping quietly into Sara's room. "Brrr...it's chilly in here," Olivia said, walking over and closing the window.

"I was breathing in the air," Sara explained. "You were right, I can smell the ocean."

Olivia smiled. "I suppose it's the wind. And there's a full moon. You know, this time of year the tides are quite high, and they're especially high during a full moon. It always seems to me that during high tide the ocean smells saltier...or perhaps it's the seaweed that washes ashore...."

"Is the moon full?" Sara asked. She was hardly able to contain herself.

Olivia continued to peek out the window. "Oh, yes it is. It's a big, full harvest moon, and it's just coming out from behind the clouds."

"Good," Sara said as Olivia blew out the lamp. Then, in the halflight provided by the lamp in the hall, Olivia came over to the bed and kissed Sara on the forehead. "Good night and sweet dreams."

"Good night, Aunt Olivia."

Sara scrunched down under her covers and waited for what seemed an eternity. Finally, she quietly got out of bed and shook herself out. She was halfway to the window when she heard more footsteps in the hall. "Aunt Hetty," she murmured under her breath, and in a flash she darted back to bed and under the heavy covers.

"Good night, Sara," Hetty ventured, standing by her door.

"Good night, Aunt Hetty."

Hetty tiptoed into the room, lamp in one hand, book in another. She set the lamp down. "I found a book you might like...it was your mother's favorite. I've been looking for it for days."

Sara looked at the book that Hetty held out. If she reached for it, her sleeve would show. "Thank you. Could you just put it there, on the table, please?"

Hetty put the book down, and then she sat on the edge of the bed. "Sara, I don't want you to think that I'm a woman without sympathy." She paused, then continued. "I realize how difficult it must be for you to come from such a sophisticated place as Montreal and come to...to Avonlea...."

Suddenly Hetty stopped and listened. "Good gracious, what was that?"

Sara forced herself to look wide-eyed. "What?" she asked.

"That noise," Hetty said, getting up and walking to the window. "It sounded like a sick dog."

"Maybe it was a wolf," Sara suggested.

"We don't have wolves." Hetty peered out into the darkness, then shook her head in irritation. "Must be one of the neighbors' dogs. I'll have to speak to them about that. I don't want strange animals wandering around in the middle of the night. They scare the chickens, and if the chickens are scared, they stop laying."

Hetty turned away from the window and returned to Sara's bed. She leaned closer to Sara. "My goodness, you're all flushed." She put her hand on Sara's head. "And so warm. I wonder if you have a fever?"

"I'm fine, Aunt Hetty," Sara said as quickly as possible.

"Maybe we should take these blankets off..."

"No! That's not it. I always get flushed when I'm tired. Nanny Louisa could tell you that."

Hetty stood up and nodded. "Well, then you must get some sleep. We can talk another time."

Hetty hesitated for a long moment, then she touched Sara's shoulder lightly. "Good night, Sara."

Sara looked up into her aunt's now soft eyes. "Good night, Aunt Hetty," she said, truly regretting that they hadn't talked. But tonight, she reminded herself, was a night that belonged to Felicity and Felix.

As soon as Sara heard Hetty go back downstairs, she got out of bed and ran to the window. As silently as possible, she opened it and climbed carefully out onto the gently sloping roof. She then crawled around to the back of the house and dropped almost silently onto the back porch roof. From there it was easy to climb down the rose trellis and into the back garden. Once on the ground, Sara began to run across the field. The moon and stars cast a light over the landscape that made it almost as bright as day.

The great orange harvest moon silhouetted the tall church spire, but the church graveyard was dark. Tall old trees surrounded it, and low rose bushes guarded it. Here, just enough light filtered through the almost leafless, skeletal trees to cast long, eerie shadows among the rows of gravestones. A light breeze whistled round the corner of the church, but it might have been the singing of ghostly spirits, Sara thought as she crept along.

"Sara," a voice hissed in the darkness. Sara almost jumped out of her skin before she realized it was Andrew. "I ran all the way, through the shortcut. They'll be here any minute." He pulled Sara down beside him and they both hid behind a huge gravestone.

Sara shivered with delight. This was the most exhilarating experience she could ever remember. She'd never been out alone at night, and she'd certainly never been in a graveyard during the full moon, either. Perhaps this was really the beginning of her grand adventure....

"I know they're coming," Andrew said, poking her in the ribs.

"I thought I'd never get out," Sara whispered. "Aunt Hetty heard you howl. She said you sounded like a sick dog."

Andrew smiled, then pressed his fingers to his lips. "Shh! Here they come." In the darkness, Felicity, Felix and Cecily came creeping to the graveyard, each carrying a lantern.

"I shouldn't have brought you," Felicity complained as she turned and looked at Cecily, who crouched behind her.

"You didn't have to bring me. You could have

just told me what was in the bag and where you were going."

"You'd have told Mama. You're just a goody-two-shoes."

Cecily ignored her sister. "What are you going to wish for, Felicity? I was going to wish for curly hair, but now I just wish I was brave. Do you suppose the bones of the dead do give off energy, like Andrew says?"

"Shush!" Felicity commanded.

"What was that?" Felix asked, terror in his voice. He stopped walking so suddenly that Felicity and Cecily almost crashed into him.

"It...it sounded like someone breathing," Felicity said, scaring even herself.

"I'm scared," Cecily wailed. "I want to go home before the ghosts come out."

"Be quiet!" Felicity again ordered. She then stood up straight and carefully opened the little pouch. She put some seeds in her mouth and made a horrible face. "Eyecch! It tastes awful."

"Make a wish, make a wish," Felix urged.

Felicity looked at the moon and trembled. "I wish I were as pretty as the lady on the cover of the *Family Guide*."

Felix screwed up his face. "What kind of wish is that?"

Sara had her hand over her mouth to keep from laughing, and Andrew smirked and rolled his eyes, scarcely able to contain himself.

"What's going on here?" an adult voice thundered out of the darkness. Felicity, Cecily and Felix were frozen to their spots.

In the moonlight, the shadow of Constable Abner Jeffries looked like a giant. He took one long side step and grabbed Andrew, who was crouched down by the gravestone to his left. "And don't you move, young lady," he said harshly to Sara, who was still by Andrew's side.

"Now," Abner Jeffries announced, "we'll all march, single file, back to Rose Cottage, where you will explain yourselves."

"This is all your fault, Felix," Felicity complained.

"My fault? I didn't even get to make my wish."

"I wish I had told Mother," Cecily put in.

"We'll march quietly," Abner Jeffries announced. "In utter, absolute silence."

It was Aunt Hetty who answered the door. Her hair, normally worn in a tight bun, was loose and tied behind her head. It looked like a horse's tail. She wore a long, full, red flannel nightgown, and over that a long, thick, wool robe.

Behind Hetty, Olivia peered out curiously. She, too, wore a long wool robe, but her hair was in two long braids.

"What in the name of Zeus is this?" Hetty said crossly as she looked at her nieces and nephews.

"Best I come inside and explain." Abner Jeffries nudged his reluctant band of prisoners forward.

At that moment, Alec King drove up in his buggy. It was obvious he had dressed hurriedly because his red flannel shirt was on inside out. "Reverend Leonard said I should come right over here." Alec King stopped and looked at his children. "What have we here?" he asked harshly as he joined them at the door.

Hetty and Olivia stepped aside to let Alec through, and then they all marched into the parlor. Aunt Hetty lit the lamp. It was as if the light loosened everyone's tongue, because they all began to speak at once.

"They threw us in the manure, so we were getting even," Andrew said.

"And they believed the seed Peg Bowen gave us was really magic," Sara said, smiling in spite of having been caught.

"I didn't!" Felicity quickly countered. "It's all their fault. They corrupted us."

"I didn't even want to come," Cecily complained.

"And I didn't even get my wish," Felix lamented.

"You dummy, you still don't understand," Felicity snapped at him.

"Ladies and gentlemen," Abner Jeffries said loudly, above the din of accusations and explanations. "If I may be allowed to speak. Frankly, the Reverend Leonard was not pleased to be woken out of a sound sleep by these vandals, who were caught red-handed in the church graveyard with lanterns and all. I must say, Miss King, I am quite tired of being dragged out of my bed at all hours to deal with your family's affairs."

Hetty stared at him, and it was plain to everyone who knew her that her anger was welling up inside. She fairly bristled.

"I'm sure you people are aware that the law forbids the desecration of church property. It's a serious offense, and one, I might add, that the law does not treat lightly." Abner Jeffries rambled on.

"We weren't des...des...a...crating anything," Felix whined.

Alec King stood up. "We've all been pulled from our beds, Abner. Dispense with the formalities so we can all get some sleep, will you?"

Hetty stood up from the piano stool where she had been perched since they'd entered the parlor. "You are quite right, Alec. This is a family matter, and Abner, it is the family that will deal with it, not the law. Now, unless you have something else to say, I suggest you go home. *I* certainly wouldn't want you to miss any more sleep on *our* account," she said sarcastically.

Abner looked from the children to Alec and then to Hetty and finally shrugged. He knew better than to argue with Hetty King. "Good night," he muttered as he beat a hasty retreat.

Alec King rubbed his chin thoughtfully. "Come into the kitchen, Hetty. I think I've thought of a proper punishment for our band of scalawags."

Hetty nodded. "And you, Sara Stanley, you go straight to bed."

Alec nodded grimly. "And you four wait out in the buggy," he said to Felicity, Felix, Cecily and Andrew.

Chapter Fifteen

The mucking-out section of the barn, into which Andrew and Sara had fallen when they were tricked by Felicity and Felix, was filled with manure, chicken feathers and hay. Raking it out and cleaning it was a smelly, dirty and very messy job. Indeed, raking it out was just the punishment Alec King deemed suitable.

Andrew wasn't dressed in his usual tweed knickers, but in faded blue overalls and a faded blue plaid shirt. Felix was dressed almost identically except for the fact that his overalls had a tear in the knee and he wore a red flannel shirt. The three girls were dressed in their oldest clothes and they all wore tall, awkward rubber boots.

"I will never forgive Father for suggesting this as a suitable punishment," Felicity complained as she took a dainty shovelful of muck and tossed it outside.

"We'll never finish if that's all you take in one load," Andrew complained, pitchfork in hand.

Felix looked at Andrew angrily. "It's all your fault. You and your magic seeds."

"You deserved it," Andrew returned.

"I wish you'd both go back from where you came, you know-it-alls," Felix hissed.

"You've made it clear since the day we arrived that you wanted us to go away." Sara looked at Felix and Felicity.

"Well, you made it clear you don't want to be here. We're not good enough for you, Miss Prissy." Felicity stared back.

"I've never said that." Sara watched Felicity carefully and wondered if that was, in fact, what Felicity believed.

"You two have caused trouble from the minute you arrived," Felicity accused.

"We have not," Andrew countered.

"And you're the ones who started it," Sara pointed out.

Felicity stood defiantly behind her shovel. "Oh, sure, Miss High-and-mighty! Flouncing around in your little lace dresses, nose in the air! Well, maybe that will change when your father's behind bars!"

Sara's face flushed with anger. "Don't you dare say that!" In a temper, she threw her own shovelful of muck at Felicity. "I would never say such a thing about *your* father!"

"Well, two can play at that!" Felicity threw her dirty hay at Sara. But it's true, she thought. Had Sara said such a thing about her father, she'd have been angry, too.

"Stop it! Stop it!" Cecily cried out. But as suddenly as she spoke, both Sara and Felicity threw hay on her. Then, for a second, no one threw anything, but all three girls began to laugh.

"Say you're sorry," Sara said to Felicity, as more muck flew through the air. And then, uncontrollably, she began to giggle.

"I'm sorry, I'm sorry. Now *you* say *you're* sorry," Felicity returned, dissolving into giggles herself.

"All right, I'm sorry too!" Sara laughed.

Andrew suddenly threw hay at Felix and Felix threw some back. In a second they were rolling and tumbling on the floor, fighting and laughing at the same time. In the haystack, Cecily and Sara held Felicity down and tickled her while stuffing dirty straw down her dress. "I'll get you!" Felicity cried out between peals of laughter.

Sara threw more straw in Felicity's face and giggled again. Never, never in her whole life had she had this kind of fun.

"Children!"

Olivia's distressed voice brought all actions and laughter to an abrupt stop. And, for once, Olivia scowled disapprovingly. Then she turned to Sara, a distressed look on her face. "Hetty just received a letter from Montreal, Sara. And there's one for you, too." Olivia held out the letter.

"It's from Papa!" Sara jumped to her feet and quickly took the letter. Its words danced in front of her eyes.

"What's wrong?" Andrew asked with concern.

Sara looked up from her letter. "My Nanny Louisa has returned to England to care for her sister, who's been taken ill. She isn't in Montreal to look after me. Papa says I can come home, but that he doesn't know how he can care for me. It says, 'I miss you dreadfully, and whether you decide to return or stay I love you always. Please have faith that we will be together soon. Papa.'"

"What are you going to do?" Andrew asked. He stopped short of telling her he wanted her to stay.

Cecily came up to Sara and took her hand. "Please stay, Sara. I'll cry if you go."

Felicity, red-faced and dirty, shuffled her feet in the hay. "She doesn't have to go. Her father said...she can stay if she wants."

Sara looked at her cousins and tried to think...there was a lot to think about. Then she turned to Olivia. "Can we go back to Rose Cottage now?"

Olivia nodded. "Certainly." Then she looked

at the others. "I'll tell Alec and Hetty. Your punishment can be continued another day. Go and
get cleaned up."

Olivia took Sara's hand and they began walking slowly back towards Rose Cottage. "Sara, it's
your decision to make, but I want you to know
that I will miss you terribly if you return to
Montreal."

"Maybe Aunt Hetty will be glad to see the end
of me. I've caused her a lot of trouble," Sara suggested. She knew it wasn't true, but she wanted
reassurance.

"Don't take Hetty at face value, Sara. She isn't
what she seems. You've got natural gumption,
and Hetty admires that. Despite how she acts, I
know she'd miss you too."

Sara looked up and realized that Olivia was
crying. She stopped on the porch and hugged her
tightly. "Don't cry, Aunt Olivia. Please don't cry."

"You do remind me of your mother," Olivia
said softly. "She had gumption, too. Oh Sara,
please stay. You belong here."

Sara did not say so, but in the barn, playing
with her cousins, she had, for the first time in her
life, felt part of a real family—a family with
uncles, aunts and children. Sara sensed that she
had been accepted, but she did not yet fully

understand her cousins. She would soon come to realize that while they would tease her as they teased each other, they would close the circle and stand as a family against strangers.

But for now she knew enough. She had felt the wonderful sensation of belonging and, truth be known, her decision was made. Sara again hugged her Aunt Olivia, then broke away from her and went inside.

Hetty was standing in the parlor. She cleared her throat. "Well, Sara Stanley, I suppose I'm losing a student. And a good student at that, as it turned out."

Sara lifted her eyes to her aunt's. "I'm staying," she announced.

"I'm sure you'll want to be off as soon as—" Hetty stopped and looked at her niece.

"I said, I'm staying," Sara repeated.

Hetty blinked at her, and Sara thought she saw Hetty's eyes misting over. "Are you crying?" she asked in a near whisper.

Hetty tossed her head and tried to look away. "Of course not! I was just peeling onions! Or maybe it's the manure. Now you listen to me, Sara Stanley. Don't you go tracking that muck all over the house. You go and get cleaned up, then come in here and pick up the things you left around this morning. Now remember, I will not stoop and carry for you...."

Sara smiled, and suddenly hugged Aunt Hetty. "I'll do my best," she promised. Then, so Hetty could not see her crying, Sara ran outside to wash at the pump.

A cool breeze rustled the wild rosebushes as she pumped out the water and washed her face and hands. She inhaled deeply and looked towards the sea. "It does smell wonderful, Mama...I think I like it here," she whispered. And then she smiled. "Your family is all right too, Mama...as soon as you get to know them."